When Church Is Over
By
Shona

When Church Is Over

© 2015 Shona Robinson by

Alicia Howard Presents

(Loyalty Ink Publications)

All rights reserved. No part of this book may broadcast in any form or without written permission for the author. With exceptions to reviewers, magazine articles, newspaper, radio host. Have my permission to quote pieces of my book for public display.

Acknowledgements

First and foremost, I would like to thank God for all that he has done, all that He continues to do, and all that He will do in my life. I would like to thank Him for blessing me with my husband Willie Robinson who has supported and listened to my ideas and let me know when I may go a little too far in a story.

I would like also thank my BFFs my Mom Willie Douglas, My loving sister Tanda Misenheimer, my twin cousin Annette Hawkins, April "Shoe Diva" Cunningham, Brian Vaulx, Vanessa Robinson, and Jeff Elrod, for all the support they gave me along the way. Even when I thought I couldn't do it and wasn't sure if I would do it they pushed and encouraged me along the way. I love you guys.

I would like to thank my family. The Nesbit Family. I could not ask for a better family. God truly blessed me when he placed me in this family. We may argue one day, but love each other every day. I would like to thank the person that read my first book and was the first person to push me to write and stick with it Ms. Lisa Silva. Thank you for letting me bounce ideas off of you. My sister from another mister Samantha Tackett, and Mr. Carl Daniel for all your support. I would like to thank Ron Rages for giving me inspiration and courage to take that next step. I would like to thank my boys Doreal, Javario and Willie Jr aka PJ, and Joshua for always being willing to do anything that they Mom requested, and my one and only baby brother Antron Nesbit.

I would like to thank my office team Ingrid Jenkins, Glenda Thompson, Jessica Bridges, Micah Johnson and Zakia Bouldin for all your support. You don't have to buy the book just because I am your supervisor, but I would highly recommend it. Lol

Last but definitely never least I would like to thank Alicia Howard presents for the opportunity, and believing in me. I would definitely like to thank Alicia Howard for teaching, mentoring and encouraging me. I look forward to learning more from you, and being a part of you moving to the next level in the publishing world.

Chapter 1

The alarm went off I rolled over to look at the clock. *"Oh shiit is 9:00 already."* Damn I don't feel like getting up out of my warm bed, but Lord knows I need to take my ass to church. Hell I am waking up cursing so you know I need to have my ass in somebody's church. I hate I had even promised Mom I would go to church with her. All I wanted to do is stay in the bed and watch lifetime all day. Hell it's not like I don't know what will happen in church anyway. Going to my mom's church is so boring. I hate going because it is so predictable. I know church is not supposed to be like a night club, but give me some excitement somewhere. Hell at least make the message good.

I took a deep breath, closed my eyes and thought about what would happen during the church service.

This usually happens at my Mom's church:

At 11:00 ushers are at the door handing out bulletins. I like to arrive after the 11:00 service has already started. Then they read the church announcements, and sing an old hymn, scripture reading, and then the choir gets up and sing. Those old songs are like listening to old Negro spirituals. I swear I could look out the window and see a black man picking cotton. They would take up tithes and offering, then the choir sings another song. Now I love praise and worship just as much as the next person, but when the choir sings there is no clapping, singing along, or dancing. Everybody just sit there, like the chosen frozen. When the choir is finished singing not one person claps they just say amen. It is exciting when I attended church where people enjoy praising, and worshipping God. Everyone praise God differently, but to sit there like a stone is unbelievable. That is not what God had in mind for praising His holy name. The speaker is usually Pastor Armstrong. By 12:00 Pastor Armstrong is up preaching, sweating, and hollering. Sometimes I see people going to sleep in church. One time I saw a Deacon sleep on the front row. I don't know how they sleep through church service with all that hollering.

Now when I go to my sister's church they sing, dance, shout, and speak in tongues. I still haven't understood that yet. My sister Amanda's church has so much energy. You never know what will happen. I sometimes wonder what made my sister go to this church because we did not grow up in that church environment. Amanda's church is not Baptist, Methodist, or Pentecostal church. The church Amanda attends is a nondenominational church which means they are not associated with any denomination. My sister puts no title on the church she attends. She says that they believe in the whole Word of God. I thought about what she said and many people say they believe the whole bible, but they are not living it. I don't believe one person or church believes in the whole bible or practices the whole bible.

I have been invited to many churches and realize that some preach what is convenient for them. With all the invites I have gotten to visit churches by coworkers, sorority sisters, or friends I realize that people don't act the same when church is over. It's like when you go to church your other personality comes out.

When we were little we went to church with our parents until we got old enough to move out and stop going. We would go every once in a while, during special occasions like Christmas, Mother's Day, Easter, Father's Day and maybe New Year's Eve with my Mom and Dad.

My older sister Amanda continued to go after we were older. While attending church with a friend Amanda joined. My Mom once asked Amanda why she joined a different church. Amanda told her she loved the atmosphere of the church. Mom just said all right. I know Mom didn't like it, but she respected any decisions we made.

I haven't been to my sister's church in two months. It seems like every time I go the pastor is preaching about me. I get uncomfortable. I hate for someone to preach at me instead of to me. His messages are doom and gloom. You go from rejoicing to tearing people down all in the same service. My sister may feel at home there but I didn't.

I turned and looked at the clock and it was 10:00. I jumped out of bed, tied my hair up, and jumped in the shower. I had already chosen what I would wear last night so I would not be running late. It's the beginning of January, and I wore a pantsuit. As I made my way out the door my phone rang.

"Hello Amanda."

"Hi Sharon, what are you doing?"

"I'm leaving for church, what's up?"

"Well I was calling to see if you wanted to go to church this morning?"

"Rain check, I am going to church with Mom today."

"Oh okay, well I'll talk to you later."

"Okay, enjoy the service."

"Thanks, have a blessed day, and I love you."

"I love you too Amanda."

As I pulled up to the church, I felt heaviness come over me. Lord I don't want to go in here. I thought, surely I will be feel better once I get inside. I looked at my watch and realized it was 11:15. When I walked in the door I felt like all eyes were on me. Immediately, I spotted my Mom. As usual she had a smile on her face, I felt a little at ease. Mom has the most beautiful smile I have ever seen. I know my Mom hates it whenever we show up late for anything especially for church, but I can tell she was glad I was here. She motioned me to come and join her. I shook my head no. I was not walking up the front of the church to sit with her. She sits like on the second row. I am disappointed that I didn't see my sister Wanda there like she promised. I called her and asked her to go with me. She told me if she could she would meet me here. I didn't see my brother Eugene either. He hardly ever went to church, and he lives with my parents. Back in the day if you lived with my parents you had to go to church, and it was not up for negotiations. But now my brother is just lies around the house sleeping or watching television. Seems like my parents are getting soft in their old age.

As church service continued I saw Sister Edna keep looking at me. All I could do is pray the same prayer I always prayed when I met that woman. *"Lord just help me keep a civil tongue, if this woman approaches me the wrong way."* Mrs. Edna" was the critic of the church. She criticize everything and everybody. That woman has something against me, because it seems she is always picking on me. Well I will try not to focus on her.

Dang the preaching is good today. I don't know who this person was that was preaching, but it sounded good from where I sat. Church seems a little different, so he must be a guest speaker. The preaching has never started this early. They usually have a lot of preliminaries.

At the end of the service they asked if there we're any visitors, if so to please stand, and give your name. My Mom turned around and looked at me. I did not move. "Mrs. Edna" was looking at me. I still did not move. Just because I did not attend regularly does not mean I am a visitor. I have not attended this church in months, but does that make me a visitor? Oh my bad I guess it does? My Mom turned to look at me so I stood and said, "My name is Sharon and I am here today visiting with my parents Mr. & Mrs. Hemphill."

I knew after church everyone would want to greet me and shake my hand, I tried to hurry out the door and get to my car. I didn't need to say anything to Mom because I would see her later for dinner.

I get halfway to my car and who do you think I see standing between my car and I? Mrs. Edna. I tried to look down as I walked to my car, so I would not be looking right at her. I figured I could just walk right pass her and act like I did not see her there. I wonder how she got out here so fast.

"Sharon!"

I hear her calling me, but I will keep walking hoping that I can get away from her, and get to my car without having a conversation with her. I will act like I don't see her.

"Sharon! Sharon!"

Lord if I could just get to the car.

"Ms. Sharon, I know you hear me gal."

Now I know I did not just hear that woman call me gal. That stopped me dead in my tracks. She must think we are still in the 1940s or something. Lord please just help me have patience with this woman.

"Hello Mrs. Edna. How may I help you?"

"I was standing here waiting to talk to you. Do you know that we are having baptism the last Sunday of March?"

"No ma'am I did not know that, but what does that have to do with me?"

"Well I see you sitting up at church today, and figured that you were serious about coming back to church. If you are I will be happy to give you bible studies and began to guide you in the ways of the Lord. If you are, you need to stop wearing those pants and start putting on some dresses. You need to start coming to Wednesday night bible study, and get serious about church. I know that nothing would make your mother happier than to see at least (one) of her children get this thing right."

It was taking everything I had plus something I did not have, not to give this woman a piece of my mind. Lord knows she needs a piece of somebody's mind because she has lost hers. I took a deep breathe.

"Well Mrs. Edna I think my Mom is happy with her children whether they go to church or not. My sister is a member of good church."

"Yeah well I have heard about that church that your sister attends. They are over there acting like church is a nightclub. They are over there dancing, and gyrating to that so called gospel music, and talking in that so called tongue language that don't nobody understands. That ain't nothing but some gibberish they don't even understand. Sharon I have known your family for many years and I feel that it is time you came back to the Lord in your own church. A church you grew up in. Your family and friends are here. Now Sharon, had you been in church you probably wouldn't have lost your husband."

Now this woman has lost her holier-than-thou mind.

"Mrs. Edna, I don't feel that you are able to talk about a situation you know nothing about. Now I am getting ready to go!"

"But Sharon I am not finished talking to you!"

"Yes…, you are!"

"Sharon I need to tell you something."

"Not me you don't."

As I drove off, I thought, that's why I don't come to church. Somebody is always there trying to give advice you didn't ask for. The woman had the nerve to say my family and friends are at the church. I have no friends here. The only family I have at this church are my parents. And she had no business talking about my marriage. Going to church had nothing to do with why my marriage failed. Neither one of us were ready to marry. We were never in love we were just in lust and once that wore off then we decided that we would part ways. We cared about one another we just didn't love each other like married people should.

I pulled into my driveway almost exhausted. My house is a colonial style home located off of South Tryon St. I love this side of town. Not a lot of new subdivisions but very nice neighborhoods are in this area. I parked my car in the garage. I need to get out here and clean this garage out soon. I went into the house to get out of these clothes. While looking in my closet to find something to wear, I thought about something a coworker once said to me. When you buy something new you should get rid of something, that way you would not overcrowd your closet. I need to get here and clean this closet out too. I choose a pair black jeans, and a white top. I looked in my drawer for a pair of white socks so I could wear my new black boots. After I got dressed I just sat on the bed. I felt so tired and drained. Church folks can take a lot out of you and deposit nothing into you. As I sat on the bed, I admired the carvings on my bed and wondered how much time it took to make these poles for my mahogany bed. I wondered who will be at Mom's house for dinner. When Mom cooks dinner someone usually stops by from the church to join them for dinner. I will call Mom to see who will be over for dinner. I picked up the phone to dial Mom's number…..

"Hello."

"Hi, Mom."

"Oh Hi Sharon, what time are you coming over?"

"That's why I'm calling."

"Oh no, don't tell me that you are not coming."

"No Mom, I was calling to see who else was coming over for dinner?"

"Baby why do you want to know?"

"Mom I don't like it when you call me baby that means you have something up your sleeve."

"What do you mean?"

"Mom what's going on?"

"I don't know what you mean."

"Mom who is coming over for dinner?"

"Just a few people." (She says whispering)

"Who's coming over Mom?"

"Well your brother will be here."

"Mom he lives there, so of course he will be there. Who else Mom?"

"Well you sister of course, Mrs. Edna, Brother Derrick, and your favorite nephew and niece will be here. You know you are their favorite aunt. The way you dote on those children makes me wonder why you haven't had children of your own."

"Mom!"

"I mean taking them out, spending time with them, and spending all that money on them."

"Mom!!"

"Yes."

"First I don't have a favorite with my nephews and nieces. Who is Brother Derrick?"

"He's a young man that recently joined the church."

"Okay, and why is he at your house for dinner? How old is this Brother Derrick?"

"He's around 32 years old. Why do you ask?"

"Mom you're not trying to set me up are you?"

"Well, Sister Edna thought that you two would have a lot in common."

"Mom, you are setting me up with someone that Mrs. Edna suggested?"

"Okay Sharon lower your voice. Now I have met Derrick and he is a nice young man. After talking with him I realized that you do have a lot in common."

"You know Mom I don't think I will be able to make dinner."

"Sharon you promised that you would come."

"Well that was before I knew that you were trying to ambush me."

"Sharon it is only dinner, it's not like it is a date."

I took a deep breath and thought about it. I wanted to see my nephew, and niece. Even though my brother Eugene gets on my nerves I still love and miss him. I also didn't get to see dad after church either.

"Okay Mom I'll be there. But Mom don't get your hopes up about a match made in heaven. And Mom do me favor."

"What is it?"

"Please have a talk with Mrs. Edna. We have already had a run in today. I don't want a repeat of this afternoon."

"What happened?"

"Nothing I couldn't handle. I'll see you a little later."

After hanging up with Mom I went into the den just to think. I took out a pen and my journal, and began to write. Writing always soothes me when I am tense and up tight. I like to just write to God, but sometimes I will write poetry.

Don't Judge Me

You don't really know me
So how can you judge me?

You don't know the real me
The person and feelings inside
You don't know what I'm feeling
Or the problems I try so well to hide

It's not your job to judge me
That job is already taken
Everyone has skeletons in their closet,
Some of us have cemeteries
And if you think you're any different
You are sadly mistaken

I know you have done things
That no one but God can see
So before you speak, just think about
Some of the things that you've done
Before you pass judgment on ME!!!!!

I pulled into Mom's driveway around 3:00. I was hoping everyone would be gone when I got there. By the look of the cars in the driveway everyone was still here. I see a gold Mercedes parked in front of the house. I figured that must be Brother Derrick's car. No one I know has a car with that loud color. The color was a little too flashy for me. I sat in the car and thought about the poem I wrote when I was at home. I can deal with many of my issues by writing in my journal. Writing "Don't Judge Me" was because of the incident this afternoon with Mrs. Edna. I wonder if I could ever get a peek into her closet. How many bones would fall out? I know that when you judge people you need to be ready for someone to judge you. I believe that it is God's job to judge not ours. Hell she probably has a whole damn cemetery in her closet.

As I walked into the house I saw Mom, Eugene, Wanda, and a strange man I guessed had to be Derrick sitting in the living room.

"Hello everybody."

"Hi Sharon, I would like for you to meet Brother Derrick McCoy."

"Hello Derrick."

"Hello Sister Sharon. Your mother has told me a lot about you."

Okay at this point I don't know what to say, because my Mom has told me nothing about him.

"That's nice. Will you please excuse me?"

"Sharon don't be rude we have company."

What is she talking about we have company. I don't live here she does so we don't have company. She has company.

"Mom, I was only going into the kitchen to see what you cooked. I am hungry."

I turned and walked down the hall towards the kitchen. He is not a bad looking guy, but looks can deceiving. I have learned the hard way, what looks good on the outside sometimes doesn't look good on the inside. I walked through the den, and I saw my nephew Terell and my niece Tawanda sitting in the den wishing they could play with the play station. Mom and Dad bought a play station and had it hooked up in the den just for their grandchildren. Mom says it is the best investment they could have ever made. Dad doesn't like them playing the game to often. He would rather see them outside playing.

"Hello sweeties."

"Hi Aunt Sharon."

"How are the two of you doing today?"

"Fine."

"Terell, how do you like middle school?"

"It is fine, but I don't like changing all those classes.

"Why not?"

"Because I get confused about A day and B day."

"What do you mean? What is A day and B day?"

"A days I have Math, Band, PE, and Reading. On B day I have Lang. Arts, Social Studies, Science, and Art."

"That does sound confusing. How do you keep up with which day it is and what books you need to carry?"

"I am usually fine during the week, but after the weekends, and Monday comes I forget what day it was on Friday."

"Well hang in there Terell you will figure it out. You are a smart young man. Do you need anything for school?"

"No thanks Aunt Sharon."

"Well call me if you need anything, and that goes for you too Tawanda. And how are you doing in school miss lady?"

"A'ight."

"Hey little girl what have I told you about using so much broken English and slang."

"Yes ma'am."

"Now how is school?"

"Fine."

"Better. Well I'll talk to you later. Call me next week so we can go to the movies."

"Okay Aunt Sharon."

I love my nephew and niece. I am just a little closer to Wanda's' children than Amanda's children, because their fathers are not around. I worry so much about T & T (that's the nicknames I gave them because I think they are dynamite children).

Wanda does not seem to do anything with her life. She is so smart and has so much potential, but she is not applying it. She says she is doing the best she can do, but we can all better with ourselves. Every day we should be a work in progress. Wanda and I are only a year apart. If I say anything to her or try to help she calls me Miss Goodie two shoes (whatever that means). I learned my lesson the last time I tried to talk to her and she told me I am no better than she is, my stuff stinks just like everybody else.

She didn't use the word stuff though. Amanda says that she is praying for her. I see no results from that either. I turned the corner and walked in the kitchen, and who I see sitting in the kitchen like she owns it…..Mrs. Edna, sitting at the table stuffing her face.

"Good afternoon Mrs. Edna."

"Hello Sharon."

I wanted to just walk out of the kitchen, but I knew that would be rude, plus I would not let this woman run me out of my parents kitchen. Hell she's the guest not me. I decide to stay I wanted to know what Mom had cooked, and then I will leave.

"Sharon."

"Ma'am."

"Did you meet Brother Derrick?"

"Yes I did."

"Well?"

"Well what?"

"What did you think of him?"

"I do not have an opinion of him one way or the other. I don't know him."

"I tried to tell you he was going to be coming over for dinner, and to tell you a little about him, but you drove off."

"Thanks for trying to warn me."

"Oh, I wasn't trying to warn you. I was just trying to make sure you would have on proper attire for a meeting with a man in his position. And look at what you chose to wear. I wish I had a chance to talk to you."

"Mrs. Edna what do you mean a man in his position and what's wrong with what I have on?"

"Derrick was a deacon at his former church in Ohio, and he is now being groomed for a deacon position at our church."

"Okay, now what does that have to do with me, and again what is wrong with what I have on."

"Well, you have on those jean britches. It's no wonder you young women today are so confused. One minute you are dressing like a man, then a woman, and then a streetwalker."

"Mrs. Edna, what are you talking about?"

"You all dress like business woman with a skirt and jacket, but acting like a businessman. Then you put on a dress, or short skirt, and revealing shirts like some kind of street woman. Then you wear a pantsuit like a man. The only thing missing is a tie. No wonder women these days are so confused; you are trying to be too many people."

"Mrs. Edna have you ever stopped to think that in nowadays women sometimes must be different people? Women must be a wife, mother, business executive, friend, lover, referee, housekeeper, chauffeur, nurse and a counselor. Being all those different people requires you to dress for the part."

"Well I just don't agree with that."

"Why doesn't that surprise me? Mrs. Edna you have a good day and I'll talk to you later."

I hope a lot later. I don't know what she is talking about, but it is time to get out of here. I am going to speak with daddy and pray that dinner is over quickly.

"Hi Daddy."

"Hi, baby. It was good seeing you in church today. How is your day going?"

"I'm fine. I just let Mrs. Edna get on my nerves."

"Baby just ignore her. Remember that she is old and set in her ways. Someone will put her in her place one day. God has a way of working it out. She is a very lonely woman. Just be patient with her and let God handle the rest.

"Alright dad, I will try, but God is not moving fast enough for me. Daddy why are you not in the living room entertaining with Mom?"

"I just need to wind down after service. I'll be in there in a minute. Do you know if dinner is done?"

"No sir, but the food looks, and smell done to me."

"Well let's go eat. I am so hungry I could probably eat one of my grandchildren. By the way where are they?

"They are in the den wishing they could play with the play station."

"Lord, they do that every time they come over.

"Dad was that a quest speaker today in church?"

"No, that is our new Pastor Josiah Brown. Come on let's eat."

Dad and I headed into the kitchen. If that is the new Pastor I might have to go to the church more often. Service was real good today and it was different.

"Dinner sure was good honey."

"Thank you Brad, would you or anyone else like something from the kitchen?"

"No honey. Why don't you sit down, and let me get you some coffee."

"Thanks honey, but I have to get the kitchen clean. Sharon, can you give Mrs. Edna a ride home."

What the hell! All I could do was look at my Mom like she has lost her mind. I don't know what possessed my Mom to even let something like that come out of her mouth.

"I'll take Sister Edna home Sister Hemphill, if that is alright with Sister Edna."

I turned to Derrick to give him a look of gratitude. This man has just scored a three-pointer. I smiled at him and got up from the table to get ready to leave.

"Dad, Mom I am getting ready to leave. Mom don't worry about the dishes I got Terell and Tawanda in there rinsing them off and putting them in the dishwasher."

"Sharon you know that I like for dishes to be washed, I don't like that dishwasher."

"Mom you have it so you may as well use it, especially when you have guest. I will talk to both of you tomorrow."

"Okay baby, be careful driving home, and thank you for coming to church today."

"Okay Mom and Dad. Goodbye everybody."

Lord I don't know how much more of that dinner I could have taken. Derrick seems like a nice young man, but I am not interested in seeing anyone right now.

Finally, home at last. Before I lay it down, I better call my parents to let them know I arrived home safely.

"Hello."

"Hi Mom, just wanted to let you and dad know that I got home okay."

"Thanks baby you know I worry about you living so far away by yourself."

"Mom I am only thirty minutes away. You make it sound as though I live out of the state."

"Sometimes it feels like you stay out-of-state."

"Mom if you would visit more often then you wouldn't feel like it was out-of-state."

"If I were invited over more often then maybe I would visit more."

"Okay Mom, I just wanted you to know that I got home."

"Okay and how did you like dinner?"

"It was fine, delicious as usual. The company was another story altogether."

"Did you let Sister Edna get to you again?"

"Yes ma'am."

"Sharon I have always told you not to pay that woman any attention. She knows how to push your buttons, and you continue to let her get to you. How did you enjoy the company of Brother Derrick?"

"I guess he was fine company. I don't know I didn't get a chance to talk to him."

"Well that is why I gave him your number for him to call you."

"Mom you did what? I can't believe you did that without asking me. What were you thinking? You don't know anything about this man, and neither do I. And you gave this man my phone number.

"I know that he is a good Christian man, and I thought you would have a lot in common. Sharon don't be mad, and please don't fuss. I have already heard enough of that from your father. I thought your father would be happy for you to have a good Christian man, but he told me to stay out of your love life."

"Dad's right Mom, take his advice and stay out of my business. When parents interfere in their children's love life it only causes problems. I'll talk to you later this week Mom. I love you."

"I love you too baby, and I apologize I did not mean to upset you."

"It's okay Mom, goodnight."

I cannot believe my mother gave a stranger my phone number. I am interested to know what the brother is talking about, but she still had no right to give him my number.

Chapter 2

I am so glad this day is almost over. Lord I don't know who whines more customers or employees. I feel like a mother of 50 bickering children, I referee and listen to bickering employees all-day. This is one of those days where I am ready to go home, turn the phone off and relax in my garden tub. Soon as I say something about turning off my phone it rings.

"Hello."

"Hello Ms. Sharon."

"Yes, who am I speaking with?"

"This is Brother Derrick McCoy. Did I catch you at an untimely moment?"

I forgot my Mom gave him my phone number. I was expecting him to call me at home.

"Not, I'm just on my way out the door, but I have few minutes. How may I help you?

"Well I hope you don't mind me calling?"

"No I don't mind. I am surprised that you would want to call me."

"Why would you be surprise?"

"You don't know me."

"That's true, but I would like to get to know you."

"Oh really?"

"Yes I would. How was your week?"

"It was fine. How about yours?"

"It was a blessed one. I was calling to ask if I could take you out for dinner tomorrow night."

"Like I said before we don't really know each other. I would feel a little bit uncomfortable going out with you and I just met you once. We have only talked twice for what seven minutes?"

"I understand. Do you mind if I call you tonight?"

"No, just give me time enough to change my clothes and relaxed."

"How's 8:00?

"Eight will be fine."

"Would you like for me to call you at this number?"

"Is this the only number that you have for me?"

"Yes. This the only number your Mom gave me."

"Yes this number will be fine."

"Well I guess I will talk to you later tonight."

"Guess so. Talk to you later. Bye."

I need to call Mom. I am glad she did not give him my home phone number. I am not ready for him or any man to have my home number.

Traffic is such a mess in downtown Charlotte that's why I leave work early on Fridays. Let's see, I need to go to the grocery store, stop at a red box to pick up a movie, and the bible bookstore.

I don't know what made me want to go to the Christian bookstore, but I just felt the need to go. Man I have never been in a bible bookstore before. There is so much in here to choose from.

After I found what I was looking for I explored the store more. I didn't realize that bibles cost so much, and that they had books on every subject you can think about. The bibles I have at home my sister and my mother brought for me when I got married. I have never brought a bible for myself.

I think I will buy one for my sister, Mom and me and have them engraved.

When I got up to the register the total came up to $300. Well I just messed up my budget for this month. I rarely spend this much on books. My budget is $20 a month for books. I love to read, but would have never thought I would spend this much. I even bought Wanda a book. I will just have to adjustment in my budget somewhere else. I felt good when I left out the bookstore.

Sunday came too soon. I must say my weekend was very nice. It's Mother's Day so I will attend church with my parents. It would be good to hear another Word from Pastor Josiah Brown.

"Church, being that it is Mother's day I have asked a guest speaker to speak today. Please make her feel welcome, Sister Michelle Cherry."

Thanks Pastor Brown for this opportunity to speak before this congregation. Good

Afternoon church, please forgive me I am a little nervous, so please continue to pray for me. I was somewhat surprised when the Pastor called and asked me to give a sermon on this day. I prayed about it and here I am. The title of my sermon is "Behind Every Good Man is a Great Woman." I know women don't like to hear that; stating they will not be behind no man, but honey I am here to tell you that's the way God wanted it to be, and I will share with you what God has shown me."

Now let us pray:

"Dear Heavenly Father please speak thru me and speak to your people. Please prepare the hearts to receive your Word. Lord I thank you for the opportunity to stand before your people. I pray that you speak through me and that I would only say what you have me to say. In Jesus name I pray Amen."

Okay now let's get into the word. Let's turn to Genesis 2:18-25.

In verse 18 God said "It is not good that man should be alone I will make him a help meet for him." In this verse the word help meet, or help mate indicate that God made woman to help man, not to hinder, tear down, push back, or push them out of the way. In the next two verses you see God create from the ground every beast of the field and every fowl of the air, and brought them to Adam to name. Our God is so awesome, and considerate. Adam didn't have to come to God. God brought all the animals to Adam to name. It shows that God had a lot of confidence in

Adam to name all the animals, but it wasn't really confidence God had breathed His spirit into Adam so he was capable of the job, (but that's another sermon). God puts Adam into a deep sleep, and took a rib and from that rib made a woman. As a woman realize that a part of us comes from man. This message can go both ways, Men you know that women come from a part of you so how can you degrade women how some of you do? See God works smart not hard. When he created man he really created them both at the same time. He didn't just create one person he created many they just have to be pulled out of you.

I'm speaking to all women. It is not bad to be behind a man. You were created just for that. That is why man was first then woman was pulled out of man. Sometimes for men to get to that next level they need that nudge or push. How are you going to push your man to the next level if you are standing beside him? You are just pushing him sideways. Sometimes that is our mentality, the crab mentality walking sideways instead of forward, and the sad part is we really think that we are going somewhere.

Now if you place yourself in front of man (which is out of order) you cannot push him to greatness if you are ahead of him. It doesn't matter if you make six figures and he is barely making $20,000 a year you still must stand behind, and whisper words of encouragement in his ear, for him to reach the level that God has for him.

Sometimes as women we are afraid that if a man reaches his full potential and reach the next level he will no longer want us. Sometimes that happens, but know that you have done what God has purposed you to do.

Remember God created man and woman but he pull woman out second. Second can't come before first, that would be out of order and we know God is a God of order. God did not make man first with nowhere to place him. He made earth and then made man and placed him in the garden. You wouldn't buy all your materials to build a house and then purchase your land. Better yet would you get satellite cable and not have a television. How are you going to watch it? We need to continue to do things decent and in order and trust God will bless.

A lot comes with being a great woman. You have to be strong to put up with a lot of the mess men put you thru. I don't mean just husbands, and boyfriends. I am talking about all men young and old whether it is your sons, nephews, brothers, friends, etc.

But as women we have to know when to let a man be a man. That means let your guard down sometimes and let the man take control. The man is supposed to be the head, don't take that away from them. There is such an outcry for men to take their place. Sometimes they can't because we as women are standing in their way. We are to encourage and uplift all men, especially our young men such as our sons, nephews, cousins, and the children in the neighborhood, they might not be getting that encouragement at home. By no means does that make a woman weak in any area of their lives. We are not stronger than men in strength, but we are stronger in endurance.
In closing please start or continue to pray, push, and stay positive for men to reach the next level. Continue to stand behind them and whisper words of encouragement to them.

Boy this week has been rough. Its spring and many people in my department are taking days off, or calling in sick. It seems more people are sick in the spring and summer than in the winter.

"Hello."

"Hello Sharon."

"Hi Mom, what's going on?"

"Oh nothing, I am just calling to see how your week went?"

"It was fine, a little stressful, but everything is okay. How's dad?"

"He's fine. He has been working on a project for the church. He won't tell me what it is."

"Mom, he's probably not supposed to say anything right now. Tell him that I asked about him."

"Okay sweetheart. By the way how are things going between you and Derrick?"

"Fine, he is a nice guy Mom."

"You have been dating for a while. People at the church keep asking me how serious you two are. Do you and Derrick have any plans for marriage?"

"How can people be asking those kinds of questions? We have only been dating for four months."

"I know Sharon, but you have been going to church every Sunday since you met him. Plus that's the most you have been to church since you left home."

"Mom I was going to church. I just wasn't attending your church."

"Are you attending church because of your relationship with Derrick?"

"I don't know Mom. Maybe that's part of the reason."

"Well I am just happy that I get to see you every Sunday. And you know your father is happy that he can see you every Sunday at church also."

"I'm happy I get to see Daddy too. Thanks for calling Mom, but I got to go. I will talk to you later.

"Brad I talked to Sharon today."

"Oh yeah. How is my girl doing?"

"Both her and Derrick are doing just fine."

"Now Laura I want you to quit pushing those two together."

"Why not Brad? Don't you want our daughter to be with a good Christian man? Brother Derrick is a good man."

"I'm not saying he is not a good man, but Laura you don't know anything about him."

"I know all I need to know. If he is good enough to be a deacon at our church then he has my vote to date our daughter."

"Laura he is not a deacon in our church yet. He was nominated."

"Well who recommended him to be a deacon in our church?"

"Laura you know that I can't tell you that. I do know that you need to stay out of our daughters' love life. Do you understand me?"

"Yes Brad."

"Good. Now I have to go. I will talk to you later. I love you."

"I love you honey."

As my husband walked out of the door I was thinking about what he said about us not knowing him. I know Sister Edna told me he was a deacon at his last church. No church would make a man a deacon if they didn't think he was a good man. I wonder why he is not still at his church and what made him move to North Carolina.

"Walking the Path Baptist Church how may I serve you today?"

"Yes, this is Deacon Hemphill at One Love Baptist Church."

"Yes Deacon Hemphill how may I help you?"

"Well I need to speak with your Head Deacon, Elder, Pastor, or someone that can give me a character reference for one of your former members."

"Hold on one moment please."

"Hello, this is Pastor Sharp how may I help you Deacon Hemphill is it?"

"Yes Pastor Sharp I am calling to get a character reference on a Brother Derrick McCoy."

"Well Deacon Hemphill this is unusual. I have never had anyone call me about a character reference before."

"I apologize if I have inconvenienced you in any way."

"No, it's alright I was caught off guard by your call."

"I understand. I also understand if you don't want to give me a character reference on Brother McCoy."

"Well Deacon Hemphill what I can say is that Brother McCoy is a man that likes to serve. He will work hard for the ministry. Due to some bad spiritual and natural decisions we could not keep him on as deacon at the church. He has great potential. This church was not the right place for him to be mentored to become a leader God intended for him to be."

"Thank you Pastor for your honesty as well as your discreetness, but may I ask you one more question?"

"Sure."

"How long has Brother McCoy been gone from your ministry?"

"About three years now."

"Do you know where he attended church after that?"

"No sir I don't."

"Thank you Pastor Sharp. I won't take up any more of your time. I appreciate you taking the time to speak with me today."

"It was no problem at all Deacon Hemphill. I hope I was of some help to you."

"You were helpful thank you, and have a blessed day."

"You to and God Bless."

Brother McCoy has only been at One Love Baptist church for a year. I wonder where he spent his other two years. And why did he give Walking the Path Baptist Church as his last church location. Where did he go to church for the last two years? Something doesn't feel right.

"Lord I pray to you today that you give me revelation on this situation. Lord please, please continue to guide me in the right direction. Lord I thank you for your grace and mercy. Lord I will be so careful to continue to give you all the praise honor and glory. In Jesus name Amen."

Chapter 3

I'm almost finished getting dressed. Derrick will be here at 7:00pm to take me to dinner. I don't know why I am so nervous. Derrick and I have been dating for five months now.

Derrick called this afternoon to make sure we were still going to dinner. He said he was taking me somewhere special tonight. I'm hoping that he is taking me to his place for dinner. The whole time Derrick and I have been dating I have never been to his place. I don't even know what side of town he lives on. I have been wanting to ask him about it, but I didn't want to seem pushy. But enough is enough. It is time for me to push.

I was a little disappointed when we pulled up at Lake Norman. I was really hoping that he would take me to his place. Derrick got out of the car grinning from ear to ear.

"Surprise, I booked us a dinner cruise. I bet you have never been on a dinner cruise before have you?"

"I have been on a dinner cruise before."

"With whom?"

"What difference does that make? It's not like you know the person anyway. I didn't even know you back then. Besides I have been twice. I went with my family once and a friend another time.

"Where else have you been?"

"Derrick what is wrong with you? Why are you acting so upset?"

"Because I tried to surprise you with a dinner cruise and come to find out you have already been on one before. I just wanted to know what else you have done just in case I want to surprise you again. Have you ever been on a cruise, flown on an airplane, or been out of the country?"

"Well if you had asked I would have told you I had been on one before. Derrick this is getting ridiculous. I think it would be a good idea if we just order our food."

"No just answer the question."

"Okay, yes I have been on a cruise, and before you ask it was to Jamaica. Yes I have flown on an airplane before. That is the only way to travel for me. I have flown to other countries. Two friends and I went to Europe right after we graduated from college. Now are you satisfied?"

I don't know what the hell is wrong with Derrick, but I would not lie to him just to stroke his ego. What kind of woman does he think I am? Does he think that I just work and sit at home all the time? Since the atmosphere is already tense I may as well ask him about not knowing where he lives or why we never go to his house.

"Derrick may I ask you some questions?"

"Sure."

"Why is it that I have never been to your house?

"Because my house is being renovated, and I just didn't want to bring you into that mess. I thought I told you that one time."

"No you never mentioned it. So you mean to tell me that your house has been under renovation for the last five months?"

"Yes it has. I am not taking you over there with all that mess. I don't want you to get hurt."

"I don't mind a little mess. I just want to see where you live."

"Well I mind. Sharon you will know where I live soon. I hope you and I will share the same address one day."

I didn't know what to say. I just sat there with my mouth open. Was this a proposal, or was this his way of letting me know that he is interested in going that direction with our relationship. It could have been his way of just changing the subject. It still bothers me I don't know where he spends his time all week, or what side of town he even lives on. Let's just get thru this dinner cruise.

I'm at Wanda's house picking up T & T. I can tell they know that I am here, because I hear their footsteps running to the door. My sister has a nice house. Section eight sure has moved up from back in the day. I had friends whose mom was on section eight when I was in junior high and they lived nothing like my sister.
"Hi, Aunt Sharon."
"Hi sweetheart. Are you ready to go?"
"Almost."
"Okay go ahead and finish getting ready. Where is your Mom?"
"She's in the den talking to her friend."
My sister really has this place looking nice. Wanda has always been good with coordinating colors, and putting

things together. Hampshire Hills is a good neighborhood, or at least it use to be, and the schools in this area are good. Right now T & T goes to Cochrane middle school, so far no problem with school, or teachers. Let me go in here and speak to my sister.

"Hi Wanda, how are you?"

"Hey Sis, I'm fine. Sharon this is my friend Shelia, Shelia this is my sister Sharon."

"Hi Shelia, it's nice to meet you."

"Girl as I was saying I thought I had died and went to heaven. We pulled up at Lake Wylie and there was this big boat sitting out there."

Did this chick just act like I didn't just speak to her? I hate ghetto minded women.

"Really, what were ya'll there for? Did he bring you up there to see the boat sail around the lake or something?"

"No Ms. Thang, it was dinner cruise. We had dinner on the boat while we sailed around the lake. They served us a nice expensive dinner. They had a band and everythang on the boat. Ms. Sharon have you ever been on a boat before?"

"Yes I've been on a dinner cruise a few times, and so has Wanda"

"My sister has been on more than just a dinner cruise. Sharon has sailed to different islands."

"Yeah, but has she every had a man take her on a dinner cruise before?"

Now what is this heifer trying to say? Why is Wanda pacifying her, she knows that she has also been on a dinner cruise before. Our father took us on a dinner cruise before, but it was at Lake Norman.

"Yes, I have had men take me on a dinner cruise before."

I just stood there looking at her like she was crazy. I hate ghetto bum bitches. Sorry Jesus. God has his work cut out for me because I am just not there yet. I can't believe that my sister is friends with someone like her. Wanda may act ghetto sometimes, but she does not have ghetto mentality.

"Anyway, girl you know that I had a good time. I have never had a man treat me that good before. I know that he spent a lot of money on this dinner, and when we got back to my place I made sure that I showed him how much of a good time I had. Girl I rocked his world."

"We're ready Aunt Sharon!"

"Okay let's go. Wanda I will be bringing them back later on. I'm just taking them to the movies and we might do a little shopping. Goodbye Shelia."

"Alright, Terrell, TaWanda I want ya'll to behave yourselves for your Aunt Sharon, and have a good time."

"Okay Mom, bye!"

"Hey baby."

"Hi Derrick, how was your week?"

"It was fine. You know that I have been in meetings all week. How was your week?"

"It was fine had a few issues come up in my department, but it was nothing I couldn't handle. I couldn't wait for the week to be over so I could see you. I hate not talking to you Derrick, or seeing you all week."

"I know baby, and I missed you too."

"That's nice to hear, I was beginning to wonder, by the time Thursday came that you did not want to talk to me."

"Don't think like that I always want to talk to you. I just sometimes don't have time to call you, but I am calling right now."

"Yeah, and it is nice to hear your voice. Are we going out to dinner tonight?"

"Yes I thought that we could go to Macaroni Grill on WT Harris Blvd."

"Sounds good to me. What time will you be here?"

"I'll be by your place around 7:30."

Derrick has been acting a little nervous ever since he arrived at my house. I leaned back in the seat and relaxed a little. I-77 seems clear tonight.

"Derrick may I asked you a question?"

"Yeah sweetheart go ahead."

"Why do we drive my car all the time? Don't get me wrong I don't mind (Lord knows I don't mind. His car is a little too flashy for me), but if we will be driving my car I could just come and pick you up from your house (where ever that may be)."

"A real man would not have a woman come and pick him up."

I wonder why we are passing the WT Harris exit to go to Macaroni Grill.

"Derrick where are we going? I thought you said we were going to Macaroni Grill."

"We were, but I decided to take you to your favorite restaurant Olive Garden. We can go to Macaroni Grill if you have never been."

"It doesn't matter where ever you want to go."

"Have you ever been to Macaroni Grill?"

"Yes I have."

"I should have known."

"Derrick we are not going to start this again are we?"

"No."

I don't know what's wrong with this man. He seems to get upset whenever he finds out the things I have done, or the places I've been. I just don't understand.

As we pulled up at Olive Garden the parking lot was not that full, but it is only 8:00. I am glad it's not crowded, the service is usually better. I have to say that the times I have come here the service was always great. As we are being seated Derrick seems nervous or something. Something doesn't seem right with him tonight.

"Sharon can you excuse me a minute?"

"Yes, but Derrick where are you going?"

"I am going to the bathroom. I'll be right back."

God I don't know what is wrong with him, but if it doesn't get better I will ask him to take me home no matter how much I miss him, or how much I like Olive Garden.

"Derrick is everything alright?"

"Well I do have something that I need to talk to you about."

Okay now I am getting a little nervous. He sounds so serious.

"Well Sharon you know that the bible says a man that findeth a wife findeth a good thing. I think that I have found a good thing with you. Before you speak all I am asking you is that you think about what I am getting ready to ask you."

Oh my God!! I sure hope this man will not do what I think he will do which is ask me to marry him. Lord I don't know enough about this man for him to be asking me to marry him. Oh my goodness he is reaching into his pocket. Okay let me calm down and stop being so dramatic. I can handle this. Just breathe Sharon breathe.

"Sharon I know that we have only been dating for nine months now, but I feel like you are the woman that God has destined for me to be with. Now I know that this is sudden, but will you marry me? But before you answer all I ask is that you promise to think about it, and that you wear this ring while you consider the proposal."

I don't know what to say. I just sat there with my mouth hanging open. I guess it wouldn't hurt to think about it.

"Okay, I promised to seriously think about it."
"Will you wear the ring while you think about it?"

Now this man is pushing it, I thought until he opened that ring box. Oooooo it was a beautiful ring. It is the style of ring I can really can get use to wearing. It is a solid gold band with what looks like a 2 carat princess cut diamond. I would rather have a platinum band, but this is really, nice.

"I don't know Derrick. I don't think that would be fair for me to wear your ring and I haven't given you an answer to the proposal yet."
"Please Sharon it would be an honor for you to wear this ring while you are considering my proposal."

"Okay Derrick."

"Good now let's eat."

"Hello."

"Sharon!"

"Mom, why are you yelling?"

"Sharon I am so hurt."

"Mom what are you talking about? What did I do?"

"Sharon how come you didn't call me to tell me that you and Derrick are engaged to be married?"

"Mom, we are not engaged."

"So Derrick didn't ask you to marry him?"

"Yes he did."

"And did he give you a ring?"

"Yes."

"I don't know about you, but where I come from we call that being engaged."

"But Mom I didn't give him an answer. He asked me to wear the ring while I think about his proposal."

"Sharon it is not fair for you to leave him hanging like that."

"Mom I'm not leaving him hanging."

"Oh yeah, then when do you plan to give him an answer?"

"I don't know. And how did you find out about this anyway. He just asked me last night?"

"Last night! You mean that Derrick just proposed to you last night?"

"Yes."

"Well Mrs. Edna called me last night to tell me. I wonder how she knew."

"Mom what time did Mrs. Edna call you last night?"

"I don't know, maybe around 7:30. I tried to call you last night to talk to you, but you did not answer."

"Derrick and I went out to dinner last night. We did not get to the restaurant until 8:30. So how did Mrs. Edna find out about it before he even asked me?"

"I don't know sweetie maybe I got the time wrong. You know how Mrs. Edna is, she can smell gossip a mile away."

"It's alright Mom. I'll talk to you later."

"Hello Derrick this is Sharon. I know that you don't like to be disturbed on Saturdays, but please call me soon. I need to talk to you before you pick me up for church."

I've been sitting waiting for Derrick to call me. Now he has to check his messages at least one time throughout the day. Thinking about this situation with Mrs. Edna has me also thinking about Derrick's marriage proposal. How can I agree to marry someone I don't really know? I don't know where he lives, or where he spends his time. We have never express feelings of love to one another. I can't marry someone I don't know. Where did he live before he moved to Charlotte? What about his family? I can't marry a man and I have never met his family. That would be crazy.

Just sitting here thinking about this situation is driving me crazy. I will just have to tell Derrick there is no way we can get married. I don't love him the way a woman should love a man she is about to marry.

"Sharon are you ready for church yet?"
"I'm sorry I'll be ready in a minute. I stayed up all night cooking dinner, and I over slept."
"Why are you cooking? Aren't we going over to your parent's house to eat after church?"
"No I thought you and I could have dinner here. I believe we have a lot to talk about."

"Like what?"

"For starters I don't feel I know enough about you."

"Is this about knowing where I live? I told you that you will know where I live soon enough. What is it that you think I am trying to hide from you? What is it that you are accusing me of?"

"I don't know what it is that you are trying to hide. I am not really saying that you are hiding anything, but you have to understand that it is not just about where you live, it's about knowing you."

"Okay we can talk about this some other time were going to be late for church, and you know that does not look good."

Chapter 4

As I continued to get ready for church I felt I would not get the answers I was seeking today. But I tell you one thing I will get answers today. Even if I don't get all the answers, and will know more that I know now.

I would like to say two things before the end of service today. As the Pastor of this church I would like to say I appreciate each and every one of you. Some of you have noticed some of the changes that the ministry is going through. All the changes made are to better the ministry. There are some exciting programs to come!

We will hold a promotional ceremony in the next coming months. I will give more details about in the coming weeks.

For those wondering what a promotional ceremony is, let me explain. When people are promoted in the spirit it is only natural they are promoted in the natural. We will ordain two people to their new position in the ministry. We will pray over these individuals and acknowledging them in front of the congregation. We want to show our support for them. Now I will have Deacon Hemphill close us out in prayer.

"Hi Mom, what is going on?"

"Hello sweetheart, what are you talking about?"

"Mom every time I turn around some woman in the church is pointing and whispering. Is my dress on backwards, slip showing, or is something hanging out of my nose. I don't understand why I am the center of attention to some people."

"I don't know sweetie. I think the word has spread that you and Derrick are engaged. Some of the women in here were hoping that they would be the one that landed him."

"Well they still might have the chance."

"Sharon what is that supposed to mean? What are you saying? Are you going to turn down Derrick's proposal?

"I don't know yet Mom. I won't know until Derrick and I have sat down and talked about several things. I'll talk to you about it later. These people are starting to get to me. You wonder why I don't attend church as much as I do. Church Folks, they are messy, hypocrites, that gossip and talk too much when church is over, and I don't have enough patience for them."

"Alright Sharon, but let me say this before you go. All people that attend church are not like that. When you come to church you come to render service to the Lord. Sharon remember it's all about Him. It is not about you, me, or church folks. Regardless of how people act you still must love them. When you come to church you pay too much attention to people and what they say. They may not act like Christians outside of the church walls, but remember when church is over God still sees all."

"I know Mom. I love you, and tell Dad I said hi, and I loved his prayer. I will talk to you later."

As I was leaving, I saw Derrick talking to Mrs. Edna. I need to talk to her anyway. As I made my way over to them I saw Derrick glance my way and he walked towards me. I tried to walk pass him so I could talk to Mrs. Edna, but he stopped me.

"Hey baby come on lets go."

"Baby I need to talk to Mrs. Edna a minute."

"Well can't it wait until another time?"

"I guess so."

The Lord must truly be working on me, because two months ago I would not have cared where I was, and I definitely would have spoken to Mrs. Edna about the mess she starts. I will let it go for now. At least I will get to talk with Derrick.

"Derrick are you ready to eat?"

"No. I am tired and I just want to lie down and rest."

"Derrick why are you so tired on Sundays? You rest and study all day on Saturday at least that's what you tell me.

"Sharon what are you trying to say? I did not come over here to argue with you. We should be over your parent's house with the other guest that were invited. Do you know that the Pastor is over there today? It would not hurt for us to go over for a little bit."

"Yes it would. How do you know the Pastor is over there?"

"That doesn't matter how I know I just feel that we should be over there. You usually spend Sundays over your parent's house."

"I tell you what we can go by there once we get our talk out of the way."

"Okay. You know that I need to be over there. You know that I am trying to be a deacon in the church."

"What does that have to do with us?"

"Nothing, what is it that you need to talk to me about? What is the problem now?"

"Okay, first of all what is up with you and Mrs. Edna?"

"What do you mean? Are you jealous of Sis. Edna? Come on Sharon I don't like women that old."

"Derrick I am not laughing. How does she know so much about our relationship?"

"I don't know what you are talking about Sharon. Sis Edna is an old lonely woman that needs attention sometimes. She does not know about our relationship. Maybe she is getting it from your Mom. You know old women love to talk. They have nothing else to do."

"She is not getting it from Mom. How did she know about your marriage proposal before you had even asked me?"

"I don't know. Why don't you ask her? How do you know that she knew before I even asked you?"

"Mom called me soon as I got home from the restaurant to ask me why I didn't tell her about the marriage proposal. I asked her how she knew she told me Mrs. Edna.

"Like I said Sharon you are going to have to ask Sis. Edna."

"Trust me I will when I get the chance. It will be a lot of things I will be saying to that lady when I talk to her."
"Sharon calm down it is not that serious. You are making a big deal out of nothing. Don't go disrespecting that woman, she is your elder. Why would you think I would know how she found out?"
"I don't know Derrick you tell me. You are the one with the secret life."
"Sharon I don't know what you want me to say. I am not going to entertain this line of questioning. You make me feel like I am on trial. Should I call a lawyer?"
"Well if it gets me to the truth, you do what you need to do. Because I will definitely do what I need to do."
"I think it is time for me to go. I do not want to argue with you. I think we need time away from each other. It will give you a chance to think about our relationship and my marriage proposal."
"So Derrick you're telling me that you are going to leave so you don't have to answer my questions. How am I supposed to consider your marriage proposal when I know nothing about you? I have been seeing you for almost a

year and I still don't know any more about you than when we first went out."

"Okay Sharon what is it that you want to know?"

"First of all where do you live, and when am I going to be invited over? Where exactly are you from? Have you ever been married? If so what happen to the marriage? Do you have any children? Have you ever been convicted of a crime? What is your credit score? What are your long term goals for the future?" When do I get to meet your parents and family?

"My mother is dead, and my father was never a part of my life! Now are you happy?

"No I am not happy that your mother is no longer living. I don't understand why you wouldn't tell me this from the beginning. What about the other questions?

"You mean to tell me not knowing my address will cause you to turn down my proposal?"

"You damn right!!!!"

"Like I said I am going to give you time to calm down and think about us and my marriage proposal. I will call you later."

"No you will not call me later. Once you leave my house don't call me anymore. Here is your ring. I can't marry someone I don't know, and who is not willing to share their past with me. If you are not willing to share your past how are you going to share your future? I will not start a relationship with you or anyone else on secrets and lies."
"Okay Sharon if you sure that is the way that you want it. Goodbye."
I don't know what is wrong with Sharon. Why she can't just except the proposal and marry me. I am not a bad looking brother if I my say so myself, but damn she ask to many personal questions. She wants my history since I was in diapers. Hope this is her ringing my phone now realizing what a big mistake she has made.
"Hello."
"You over to the Hemphill's yet?"
"No. I am on my way there now."
"Sharon is with you right?"
"No. I left her at her house."
"What? Boy are you crazy? People must see the both of you together."

"Well actually she gave me back my ring and told me she did not want to see me again."

"You need to get back to her and straighten things out with her!"

"No. I am going over to the Hemphill's house. This might be my only chance to get a one on one with the Pastor. I will work things out with Sharon later."

"Listen if you expect to get the position in the church that we both think should have you will need her on your arm, so go straighten things out with Sharon!"

"Listen Auntie I got this one. Just let me handle it."

"Okay. We will do it your way, but you will wish you listened to me."

Well I guess that's it. I thought I would be fine with my decision. I would be lying if I said it didn't hurt just a little. I never considered myself engaged, but I will miss talking to him and spending time with him. I won't miss the secrecy, or the lying. Now I haven't technically caught him in a lie, but he was not being one hundred percent truthful with me. Not that people are truthful with each other because the Bible says only a fool tells his whole heart, but

I didn't feel that Derrick was being at least 25 percent truthful with me. That's probably Derrick calling me now.

"Hello."
"Hey baby is everything alright?"
"Yes Mom why do you ask?"
"Well Derrick is over here and I asked where you were and he said he had to drop you off at home because you said you were not feeling well."
"Mom I'm feeling fine."
"Then what's this about you not feeling well."
"Mom I feel fine I promise. I will talk to you later."
"Okay baby, I love you."
"I love you to Mom."
Now I wonder what that was all about. Why would Derrick go over to my Mom's house, and further more why would he tell them I was not feeling well? Something is not right with him, and in time all will be revealed.
"So Derrick, how has your stay been in Charlotte?" Have you adjusted well in the church, and in the area?"
"Yes Sir Pastor Brown. I have enjoyed the new direction the church has been taking, and I'm looking forward to

being a part of the changes that will take place at One Love Baptist Church."

"That's nice to hear son. What kind of ministry are you interested in, or better yet what has God gifted you to do? How active were you at the last church you attended?"

"I was very active. I was deacon at the last church I attended."

"What was the last church that you attended?"

"I thought I told you Mr. Hemphill. It was Walking the Path Baptist Church."

"Oh I apologize. You told me that. So you were a deacon, and what else did you do?"

"Well I started up an awesome youth program. We had many activities going on with the youth under my leadership."

"Well that's nice to hear. Are you looking to work with the youth here?"

"I'm looking forward to being where ever I am needed. Where ever God has deemed me to use my gifts then that is where I will serve. I believe God has gifted me to work with the youth."

"You do? Now tell me how you feel that God has gifted you to work with the youth. What kind of gifts do you have that would qualify to work with the youth?"

"First of all I have worked with the youth before so I have experience. I am very relatable with young people. I like to listen to them and not so much dictate to them. Instead of giving them the answer to all of their issues I guide them in a direction of coming up with their own solution."

"Sounds good Derrick sounds real good. That's what I like Brad a willing servant. Brad you need to set up an appointment for Mr. McCoy to be interviewed by you and I sometime soon. I would like to get him working on some programs here. Do you have any children of your own?"

"No sir, Pastor Armstrong, but I hope to one day have some."

"Well son you are not getting younger. Is there a young woman you are courting?"

"Yes sir. I am courting Deacon Hemphill's daughter Sharon."

"Brad I didn't know that. Well from what I know about Sharon she is a good woman."

"Yes sir she is a wonderful woman. I have asked her to marry me."

"Oh really, Hemphill you didn't tell me your daughter was engaged."

"Pastor Brown this is news to me!"

"So when will you all be coming in for some counseling?"

"I don't know yet. Haven't really sat down and talked about a date. We are just trying to really get to know each other, and I am sorry Mr. Hemphill I thought you already knew."

"Okay son that is a good idea, but I hope you are not trying to get to know her to well if you catch my meaning."

"Oh no sir we both have agreed to wait until we were married before having sex."

"Good. You do not want to start off a marriage on the wrong foot."

"Well brother Derrick I look forward to great things from you!"

"Hello. Yes I just left the Hemphill's house. I had a long sit down with the Pastor. He told Mr. Hemphill we need to set a meeting and sit down and talk. He also said that he is looking forward to seeing great things from me and hearing some of my ideas I have for the youth ministry, and other ministries in the church."

"See I told you that you could do it if you just listen to me. Now you have only to straighten things out with Sharon and you are home free."

"I will work on that tomorrow. I'll send her some flowers or something and apologize. She is just too damn nosy for me. The girl thinks she has to know everything about me."

"Boy is you crazy! The girl ain't no fool! If you gonna marry somebody you best to know more than their first and last name! That's what's wrong with some heifers they don't know enough about the men they are laying down with."

"Okay, but I don't want to tell the girl my whole life story. It is not any of her business."

"Boy we are living in the computer world now if the woman really wanted to know about you she could find out. Don't be stupid and throw away everything you worked so hard to build up. I am not saying tell her everything cause you don't want to scare her off, but at least give her enough to be satisfied. I thought you young boys knew how to play the game, but I see you don't."

"What do you know about playing the game? You have been in retirement for so long that the rules have changed."

"Maybe so, but the game is still the same just the players have changed. That is the way folk play in church. God's word stays the same, only the people preaching about it changes, and if you plan to be pastoring over your own church one day then you need to listen. I have been in church a long time and I have seen people come and go and I know the politics of the church."

"Okay, well let me straighten this thing out with Sharon first and then we will move to the next step. I expect to be in that promotional ceremony in a few months. I will see in a minute."

Chapter 5

"Hi, Amanda, thank you for meeting me for lunch."

"No problem sis. I am glad we can take the time to have lunch with each other it has been awhile. We really need to do it more often, but next time we will invite Wanda to come along. Now what is it you would like to talk about?"

"How do you know that I wanted to talk to you about something? Can't I just want to have lunch with my big sister?"

"Yes you can, but girl quit playing I could tell in your voice that something is bothering you so spit it out! Is everything all right between you and Derrick?"

"No! I called off the relationship two weeks ago."

"A couple of weeks ago, and you just now telling me. What happened? What did he do? Have you told Mom and Dad yet? He didn't put his hands on you did he? Should we call some of our cousins?"

"Hold on Amanda, dang! This is why I waited to tell you. No I haven't told Mom and Dad, and no he didn't put his hands on me."

"Then what's wrong?"

"Well I just don't feel like I know enough about him to be settling down with him. He is unwilling to share any of his past with me. Amanda I don't even know where the boy lives. Now what kind of relationship is that to have?"

"Have you tried talking to him, letting him know how you feel?"

"Yes we had a big blow out. He says that he doesn't see what the big deal is about. Why do I need to know his whole life story?"

"Sis if you really what to know about him you know that we can find out!"

"Yes I know, but I want him to tell me. I don't want to have to investigate. If I have to do all that then I don't want him. That's the way I feel now. I shouldn't have to keep begging him to talk about his past."

"You're right, but have you heard from him since the blow up?"

"Yes. He keeps calling and leaving messages on my voice mail at least once a day. He has sent flowers to my office and my home."

"So what are you planning to do? You cannot avoid him forever."

"I don't know Amanda." I gave him a choice to talk or leave. He left and I gave him back his ring. I think that is all self-explanatory."

"Do you love him?"

"I don't know. I do like him, but I can't say that it is love."

"Girl if you have to think about it then it is not love. Listen are you sure you are not pushing him away because of what you went through with your first husband? I know Rashon hurt you but you have got to give love another chance. Now I am not saying give Derrick another chance, but I am saying that when God finally sends you the right man you have got to open up your heart and let him in. I don't know how you are going to feel about this, but I am going to say it anyway. Just take time out for you and God right now. Talk to Him and ask Him if Derrick is the right man for you. And I am going to tell you right now that you are not in love with Derrick, because when I asked, you should have immediately said yes. When you really love someone you don't have to think about it."

"I feel like it is already just me and God considering that Derrick and I don't spend that much time together."

"What do you mean you don't spend that much time together you have been seeing him for almost a year?"

"We spend more time talking on the phone during the week, and we may go out on Fridays. I don't talk to him on Saturdays, because that is his time to study and seek God. We go to church together on Sundays."

"Have you had sex with him?"

"No. Derrick told me from the beginning he did not believe in having sex before marriage, I don't like it, but I had to respect it."

"What do you mean you don't like it? Be honored that he wants to wait."

"I know I should, but I would like to see what's in the package before I purchase the gift. I need to know if it will need batteries and how long the batteries will last. Yes it sounds bad, but that's just me."

"Girl you are crazy! So have you been to church since you and Derrick had the blow up?"

"No. I didn't want to run into him."

"So you were only attending church because of your relationship with Derrick?"

"No at least I don't think so. I have really come to enjoy going to church. I don't know if going was because of Derrick or not. Dad asked if I would consider working with the youth, and you know how much I love children."

"Yes I do, and I think it is a great idea. Are you going to do it?"

"I don't know. I have been giving it a lot of thought."

"Let me just say this. Pray about it before you decide, or before you commit to anything. Have you decided if you are going to church this Sunday?"

"Yes I have definitely decided to go this Sunday. I really miss church. Pastor Brown has really been preaching and teaching the word lately. I have had Mom bring me CDs of the sermons for the past couple of weeks. I have been listening to them, and I have to say I hate I missed it. Besides I have decided that I will let no one make me miss out on what God has for me. I will be in church this week listening to the sermon in person."

"Alright, now that's what I'm talking about!"

"Amanda, can I ask you a question? Do you have to deal with messy people in your church?"

"What do you mean sis?"

"You know people that are always in your business, talking about everyone in the church, hypocrites, women who come to church looking for a man and not the Man, a Mrs. Edna, etc."

"Sharon I think there are messy people in every church, but when you come to church you don't worry about those type church folks. The bible says those that are led by the spirit of God are the sons and daughters of God. You can't let church folks bother you. Understand that we are servants of God here on earth. That's why you must pray and ask God to help you find the right church home. See the bible also says that God places people in the body as he sees fit. That means when you find your home God put you there for a reason, and not to just sit. God expects for everyone to serve Him. There are messy people everywhere in and out of church. Do you understand what I am saying?"

"Yes I do. I just want to tell you thank you for listening. Your advice is always appreciated."

No problem little sis. You know that I love you, and you can talk to me anytime.

Now let's go shopping!"

"Yes, now let's go shopping so I can pick me up a new outfit for church Sunday."

I love going shopping with my sister, not only does she have good taste, but she is so fun to be with. Amanda is also a comedian when she wants to be. She was so funny today. We went to Southpark mall, and we had a ball. After lunch at the Cheesecake factory, we really did a number on the mall. Next time we will have to invite Wanda. I might just take Wanda out in the next couple of weeks.

"Brad I need to talk to you about Sharon. Now I know that you told me to stay out of it, but I feel that something is not right about her and Derrick's relationship, and with him asking Sharon to marry him I just don't know. I thought that he would be the perfect guy for her, but something just don't feel right. I tried to talk to Sharon about it but she won't talk to me about it."

"Yeah I heard from Derrick that they were engaged. I appreciate the heads up honey."

"To be honest with you, I thought you already knew. I thought there was no one in the church that did not know about the engagement."

"You know that I don't listen to church gossip. I can't say that I am happy about this, but we still have to let Sharon make her own decisions. Now I might not like the idea, but she is grown."

"But Brad you know that something is not right with him. You may not have said anything, but I know that you don't trust him. I can tell by your body language whenever he is around."

"Woman you know me so well, but like I said Laura it does not matter what my feelings are for him, Sharon is still going to have to make her own decisions."

"Okay Brad if you say so, but I still don't like it. It was good to see her in church Sunday."

"I know you don't but we have to trust her judgment. Now come over here and give your man a kiss."

"Hi Wanda."

"Hey Sharon, why did you invite me out to lunch?"

"We haven't spent any time together. I spend more time with your children than I do with you, and I felt it was time you and I spend a day together."

"Spending the day out with your sister sounds more like an Amanda and you thing."

"Amanda and I spent last Saturday together and I thought that this Saturday would be good for you and me."

"That was sweet of you. You know I am down for anything that is free. Where did you and Amanda go last week?"

"We came here to the Cheesecake factory. I figured we can go shopping after lunch."

"Sounds good to me, but you know that I don't have money like that!"

"It's alright it is my treat. I invited you. Besides I need to pick your brain about something. What would you think if you had a man, and he never took you to his house, and you don't even know where he lives?"

"I would say that he is married. Is this about Derrick?"

"Yes, I don't know why it is such a big deal, but I have never gone out with anyone and not know anything about him. Wanda I know nothing about him, and to top it off he asked me to marry him. How am I supposed to marry someone I don't really know?"

"Sis, all I can tell you is that there is something up with that Negro. Have you tried talking to him about it?"

"Yes, I actually broke off the engagement."

"You did! What did you do with the ring?"

"I gave it back. I can't keep a ring from a man I am not going to marry."

"You know what they say, what is done in the dark will come to the light. Now you know if it had been me I would have put a tail on him already. I would have had someone from the hood find out all the information I wanted to know."

"Yeah, but I want him to give me the information freely. I don't want to have to trick him, or threaten him to give me the information."

"Well ain't that what you are doing now? You have told him you wouldn't marry him unless he could tell you more about himself."

Our food had arrived and I ordered the lunch soup and salad with sourdough bread. I hadn't really noticed what Wanda had until it came to the table.

Wanda had ordered a pasta dish with chicken and a nice looking sauce. I don't like penne pasta, or angel hair pasta and that is what most of their pasta dishes are here.

"One thing that really bothers me is that whenever we go somewhere and he ask me if I have been there and I say yes he gets upset. I don't really understand what that is all about. What is wrong with him?"

"Damn I can imagine how he would act if he knew that you have traveled over half the world."

"I have not done that much traveling, but he did get mad. He asked who I went with, have I been out the country and everything. When I told him yes he caught an attitude."

"Girl I know what's wrong with him."

"What is it?"

"Girl, Derrick likes ghetto girls!"

"How do you figure?"

"Well most ghetto girls have never really been anywhere, done anything, doing a lot of traveling is out of the question. They consider traveling going down to Myrtle Beach. Most women only thinking about getting their nails done, hair done, and getting somebody to pay for their cell phone bill. Derrick has a big ego. He wants a woman to get excited over every little thing he does. It makes him feel more like a man. Some men love a damsel in distress. He likes the fact that he is the one introducing them to different things in life."

"Okay I understand now, but I don't know if that is really Derrick. If that is the case then why would he ask me to marry him? He knew that I wasn't that type woman."

"I don't know. I told you something is up with that Negro. Does Mom and Dad know that you turned down Derrick's marriage proposal?"

"No, I don't know when I want to tell them. I know Dad will be alright, because I got the feeling that Dad didn't care for him. Mom on the other hand is the one who set us up."

"Girl, you know that Mom will be alright. What makes you think Dad is not feeling Derrick?"

"I don't know it is just the way Dad acted whenever Derrick was around. I could be just imagine things."

"Probably not you know how sensitive dad is when it comes to his girls. Hey can I get a cheesecake to go?"

"Yeah sure, now let's go shopping!"

Wanda and I had a good time shopping. We went into almost every store in the mall, mostly to walk off some of this food. We went into Victoria Secrets and brought bubble bath, body lotions, and two panty and bra sets. I have issues with my panties and bra matching my clothes. No one can see it, but I can.

Chapter 6

"Hello."

"Hey boy have you talk to Sharon, and straighten things out yet?"

"No not yet. I was going to try and talk to her after church."

"What are you waiting on? You know you need to straighten that situation out. You are not going to get where you are trying to get without her!"

"I know, I know. I will talk to her tomorrow after church."

"Why can't you talk to her today so that you and her can show up together. Ya'll showing up separately and sitting separately makes people talk. People are already talking about you all have split up."

"I don't understand why I can't get the position without her. I don't need to be married to be a deacon in the church."

"Maybe not, but all our deacons are married and it looks better to have a nice looking woman by your side. Having a woman by your side takes you a long way especially a deacon's daughter. Trust me boy!"

Man that was a good sermon. Let me hurry up and get out of here before I run into Derrick, Mrs. Edna, or some other people I don't feel like dealing with. Lord look these two here look like they have just left the club. Wait they were looking, and pointing at me a few weeks ago.

"I see Ms. Thang don't have the ring on no more."

"Excuse me are you talking to me, or just talking about me?"

"Well if the ring fits, oh it must don't because I don't see it on your finger."

"First of all you don't need to be talking about things that you know nothing about!"

"Whatever, come on girl lets go."

"Sharon what's going on here?"

"Nothing Mom, I am getting ready to leave."

"Okay if you say so, but are you coming over for dinner today?"

"It all depends."

"On what?"

"Who else have you invited over?"

"No one, you are the only one I had planned on coming for dinner."

"What time do you want me to come over?"

"About 3:00."

"That's fine. Do you need for me to bring anything?"

"No, just yourself."

"Are Wanda and the children coming over?"

"I don't know. I haven't talked to your sister in a couple of days, but more than likely. You know that girl doesn't cook. She will probably drop the children off and keep going."

"I'll stop by her house on the way to yours."

"Alright I'll see you later."

Since I am only going over to Mom's house, I will put on a jogging suit. I am getting my grub on today. Darn, I meant to ask Mom what she was cooking for dinner. Oh well it doesn't matter because Mom can burn, and whatever she cooks I will probably have two helpings. I have not been eating well this week. I have been too busy.

(Knock, knock, knock)

"Who is it?"

"It's me Derrick."

"Derrick what are you doing here? And why are you coming to my house without calling first?

"Since when do I need to call first before coming over to my girl's house?"

"Since we are not together anymore. Now what can I do for you?"

"Sharon I just need to talk to you for a few minutes."

"Okay, all you have is a few minutes, I am on my way out the door."

"It will only take five minutes. Where are you going?"

"I am going over Mom's house for dinner."

"Sharon I just wanted to apologize for the way I behaved a couple of weeks ago."

"Your apology is accepted. Is there anything else?"

"Yes I was wondering if you would be willing to consider giving us another chance."

"You have got to be kidding, right? I could never consider giving our relationship a chance with all the unresolved issues we have!"

"What unresolved issues? I have no unresolved issues, and I hope you are not still tripping on where I live and not knowing my address. How can you let something like an address affect our relationship or what we have together? I thought we had something special."

"It's more than just your address. I realized that I don't really know much about you."

"You know all you need to know."

"No I don't. How can you say that? When you are about to marry someone you should know as much about them as possible."

"Well you know the bible says only a fool tells his whole heart."

"So you think you would be a fool if you tell me about yourself. I am not asking questions like how many women you have slept with, which is something that I should ask. I need answers to questions that will affect both of us."

"Sharon what would you like to know?"

"What side of town do you stay on?"

"I live in Hidden Valley."

"Have you ever been married?"

"No."

"Do you have any children?"

"No."

"What is your credit like?"

"It's alright."

"Would you be offended if I asked to see a copy?"

"Yes I would. I feel that is personal information."

"So you feel that a woman or a man doesn't have the right to know what a person's credit history, medical history, or criminal background is before they commit to a lifetime together. I made that mistake one time before with a former boyfriend, and I promised myself that I would never make that mistake again. I will never get seriously involved with a stranger."

"But I am not a stranger. We have been dating for at least a year. How can you call me a stranger?"

"Yes we have been dating for a while and I feel like I know less about you now than the first time we met. Derrick to be honest we don't know enough about each other to be committed to each other."

"Sharon I know everything that I need to know about you."

"Yes Derrick you probably do, but that's because I have allowed you access to my life. My life is not a secret so you are able to learn things about me. You have spent time with my family, we attend church together. My life has been an open book for you. Another thing, how can we even consider marriage and we have never expressed feelings of love?"

"Sharon you know I don't believe in sex before marriage."

"Derrick that's not what I'm talking about, but are you trying to tell me that you have never had sex before?"

"No that is not what I am saying. I just respect you too much to violate you and have sex before marriage."

"Ok, if you say so, but Derrick that's not what I'm talking about either. I'm talking about saying the words."

"Sharon we can learn to love each other. When the people in biblical times got married they didn't really know each other, nor did they love each other. Marriages were arranged, and because they loved God they learned to love each other."

"Dammit Derrick we are not in biblical times. We are in the twenty first century and things work a hell of a lot differently in this day and age. Are you trying to say that if I love God then I should love you?"

"Yes, that's basically what I'm saying."

"Man have you lost your mind? That is the dumbest thing I have ever heard. Look I don't really think this will work out."

"What are you talking about? You haven't given it a chance. I think we are perfect for each other."

"Derrick how would you know that? We have barely spent any time together."

"So what do you call the time we have spent together for the last year?"

"I call that very little time, when we are only spending one night a week together. That's not enough time to get to know each other."

"So are you telling me that you will not continue to consider my marriage proposal?"

"I don't think there is anything to consider."

"Well, can we still see each other?"

"I don't think that would be such a good idea. I think that it is very clear that we have different ideas about relationships."

"Maybe you are right about everything, but I can change. Can we at least still talk on the phone until you see enough of a change you would consider going out with me again?"

"I don't think so. You had almost a year. Nothing will change."

"So you really don't want to see me anymore?"

"No."

"Well it's your lost. Guess I will see you around."

"No you won't, and Derrick if you ever stop by my house without calling first you will be standing outside."

"Hi Mom, hi dad!"

"Sharon what took you so long.?"

"Derrick stopped by, and wanted to talk."

"Is everything alright?"

"It is now. Mom, Dad, I have something I want to tell you."

"What is it? We're listening."

"I decided not to accept Derrick's marriage proposal. I felt we didn't know each other well enough to be getting married, or anything else."

"Thank GOD!!!!!!!"

"What is wrong with you? Mom I thought this was something that you wanted. I know Dad didn't care too much for him, but Mom I thought you did."

"Sharon he is alright for you to spend time with, but not to marry."

"Baby girl how did you know that I didn't care for him?"

"Dad I could tell by your body language whenever he was in the room."

"My ladies think that they know me well. Let's eat! I have a big appetite now!"

I really look forward to the weekends I spend with my nephew and niece. I cannot explain the feeling I feel when we are together. I think I like playing mother to them. I know they already have a mother, but since I have no children. I have adopted them as my own on the weekends. I think that I will take them shopping for a new outfit to wear to church. "Lord if I have not thanked you before I thank you now for blessing me with such a beautiful, smart, and well behave nephew, and niece. I also would like to thank you for blessing me and allowing me to work with the youth in the church. It has really been a great joy."

(Knock, knock)

"Hello Wanda."

"Hi Sharon, the children will be ready in a minute. Have a seat, you remember Shelia?"

"Yes, hello."

"Anyway we're going to dinner tonight."

"Wait a minute Shelia did you hear my sister speak to you?"

"Yea I heard her."

"Then bitch you can speak back. You are in my house don't disrespect my family."

"Dang, okay it is not that serious hey Sharon. Now we are going to dinner tonight."

"Where is he taking you tonight?"

"Chili's, and I am looking forward to it. Girl I have never had a man treat me as good as he does. He took me to Olive Garden last Saturday. They have the best pasta I have ever had."

"Girl you act like you have never been out to eat before."

"I have, but not some of the places that he has taken me. Remember the time I told you he took me on the dinner cruise. That was the first time I gave him some."

"Has he taken you to his house yet?"

"No. he says that his house is being renovated, and besides he says that he likes spending time at my house. And girl he is the bomb in the bed, a little rough sometimes, but he will have you calling for Jesus. He told me I sure know what a man likes in the bed. Girl you know when the time comes I do my thang. I will not let no woman out do me in the bedroom."

"Girl you never told me what your friend's name is."

"Oh girl I get so excited when I talk about him I just call him my man. His name is Derrick."

I thought I was dreaming when I heard her say Derrick's name. I looked over at Wanda, and I already knew what she was thinking. I couldn't say nothing. I just wanted to get up and run out of the house. Wanda looked at me and shook her head. She must have known what I was thinking. Wanda wanted me to stay right where I was and finish listening to this conversation. One thing about it my sisters they don't play, so I knew better than to move.

"So Shelia what is Derrick's last name?"

"McCoy, why do you know him?"

Lord help me to stay grounded and silent as I listen. I know were Wanda is going with her questions. Lord I hope she doesn't go too far. I really don't wanted to know any more than I already know.

"Hello Aunt Sharon, we are ready to go."

Hello children."

"T you and Tawanda go into my room for little bit while I talk to your aunt Sharon."

"But Mom I thought Aunt Sharon was coming to get us?"

"Boy get yourself into the room and I'll be in there when I am ready for you all to come out. Do I make myself clear?"

"Yes ma'am, let's go Tawanda."

"So Shelia your friends' name is Derrick McCoy?"

"Yes do you know him?"

"I might. Tell us more about him."

"Like what?"

"Like what does he drive, what days do you get to spend with him?"

"During the weekdays he comes by my house on Tuesday and Thursday night when I cook dinner for him and he usually spends the night. We go out on Saturday nights. Why all the questions? Where do you know him from?"

"Well you really never told me much about him. You only told me some of the places he takes you."

"I didn't feel I had to tell you anything about him, because it is none of your business."

"Your right it is none of my business, but none of the other things you told me were either."

"Why such an interest in him now?"

"Because if it is who I think it is then he is a dog, and you would probably be better off without him."

"How would I be better off without him? He has spent more time with me in the last three weeks than the whole time we have been dating. He has treated me better than any man I have ever dated. He treats me like a woman and not like a ho. I am not getting ready to give him up for something that you think that you know."

"I think I had better leave. Wanda I'll go back there and get the kids. Shelia it was good seeing you again."

"You too."

"No Sharon you are not going anywhere. I hate it when men try to play women like this. Shelia the reason I know Derrick is a dog is because until three weeks ago he was seeing my sister. They have been seeing each other for almost a year. He asked my sister to marry him and she turned him down and gave him back his ring. So you see he was seeing both of you at the same time."

"I don't believe you! I am leaving. I'll holla."

"Terell, Tawanda it's time to go."

"Sharon you don't have to take them if you don't feel like. I would understand and I will just tell the children you are not feeling well."

"No, Wanda it's alright. I just wish you had broken it to her a little softer. Besides I will not let him or anyone else mess up the weekend I have plan with my babies."

"Ok, if you're sure. If I haven't told you before I really appreciate all that you do for me and the kids. I love you."

"I love you to Wanda."

Shopping is always a good relief for me. It seems to take my mind off any troubles or worries. Now I probably blew my budget on clothing for this month, but it was worth it. We all got black and white pen stripe suits, and a new pair of shoes. Tawanda and I got a pant suit, and Terell got a new suit. I even brought him some cuff links.

The children and I looked wonderful all dressed alike. Mom kept saying she can't believe how adorable we looked. Dad looked so proud. You would think that we never came to church. I have to admit we looked good. Mom invited us over for dinner, but I told her I was planning to take the children over to Amanda's house. I told her that Amanda had invited her and dad too. Mom says she will ask Dad. More than likely they will show up.

"Hello."
"Derrick did you see Sharon at church today?"
"Yes I did."
"She and those kids looked good together. That's how your family with her should look. Can you just imagine you all sitting in church together as a family. You should have made your way over there and sat with them so people can see how you would look as a family. Boy do I have to tell you everything?"
"Look, I have talk to Sharon and she doesn't want to have anything to do with me. I can't make the girl want to marry me!"

"You haven't tried hard enough! That girl is simple minded and doesn't know what she wants. It is up to you to convince her of what she wants. I know you know how to play mind games because I have seen you do it before. If you are supposed to be a so call player then play the game!"

"I am getting ready to get off the phone! Bye!"

"Hi Mom."

"Hey baby. Did you have fun with Aunt Sharon?"

"Yes ma'am. Aunt Sharon brought us a new suit and we took pictures together, and we went over to Aunt Amanda's house to eat!"

"Okay, now go put your things away. Sharon thanks again for taking them this weekend. They like staying with you."

"You don't have to thank me. I really enjoy their company. I brought you over two pictures so you can see what they looked like yesterday."

"Thanks. OMG! Are these my babies? They look so adorable, they look like they can be your kids. Thanks again for taking them yesterday, and I want to apologize for what happened this weekend."

"What are you apologizing for Wanda?"

"You finding out about Derrick the way that you did?"

"Wanda there is no need for you to apologize. You did nothing wrong."

"Well I just feel bad anyway. I tried talking to Shelia, but she wouldn't listen. She thinks Derrick is the best thing since cell phones."

"If she thinks he is so great then she can keep him."

"If you want to talk then you know you can call me. I know I am not Amanda, but I know how to listen."

"Thanks, but I'm fine. I'm not as upset as everyone thinks that I am, but I appreciate the offer. I'll talk to you later."

"Okay, and Sharon?"

"Yes."

"I love you."

"I love you too Wanda."

Chapter 7

"Alright everyone I will try not to keep you long. We will try to make this painless as possible. I know some have to get home and get ready for work, so I will try to keep that into consideration.

Sister Edna what are you doing here?"

"I come for the meeting Pastor."

"You are not an elder or deacon, and I thought I made myself clear on that subject. We will have a meeting with the leaders later on this month."

"I thought this meeting is about changes that are going to be made in the church."

"It is, but there are other things that need to be discussed here. Any changes made will be discussed with the church members at a later date."

"Well I volunteer from time to time and I help out the deacons, elders, and I am a deaconess."

"Well Sister Edna we do appreciate everything that you do at the church, and I know that God is pleased with your serving, but again this meeting is strictly for my deacons and elders in the church."

"If this meeting is about church business and changes in the church then I feel like I have a right to be here. I am a heavy tither in the church. My husband was head elder in this church before you even got here. My family and I have donated a lot of time and money into this church, and I feel I have a right to stay for this meeting. The former Pastor use to let me stay for all the meetings!"

"Okay can I have everyone to meet in the conference room? Miranda has refreshments, pen, pencil, and paper set and ready to go for the meeting.

Sister Edna how about we meet at a later date you, me, my wife, and one of the other elders of the church? I will answer and discuss any concerns at that time. Miranda when is my next available appointment date?"

"The next available date is March 19th @ 1:00pm."

"Thanks Miranda. Is that good for you Sister Edna?"

"No, why do I have to wait until later? And why does Miranda get to stay she is not an elder or deacon?"

"Actually Miranda is my personal secretary, and she is not staying. She is just here to make sure that I have everything needed for this meeting. Now if there is not anything else I will speak with you on March 19th @ 1:00 pm. Now we really must get this meeting started."

"Alright Pastor Brown I'll wait until the 19th, but I have a lot to discuss with you. Miranda I need a ride home please."

"Okay Sister Edna, I'll give you a ride."

"Everyone I apologize for the interruption, now let's get on with the meeting so we can all get back to our families. Elder Clark would you open us up in prayer?"

"Dear Heavenly Father we come before you today as humble servants. We thank you for bringing us together tonight, and we pray that we can be on one accord. We continue to ask for your spiritual guidance. We continue to pray for spiritual, physical and financial blessings over our pastor, his family, and this ministry. Lord we thank you for wisdom, we thank you for understanding, and we thank you for unity in Jesus name we pray. Amen"

"Thank you Elder Clark for that much needed prayer. The atmosphere is now appropriate to begin the meeting. We have appetizers prepared for you, and Sister Hemphill will be along in the next hour to bring dinner. I understand that some of you are coming straight from work and haven't had time to stop for dinner. We also have paper, pens, and pencils so you can take notes."

"Like I have stated before we are here to do some restructuring in the ministry. Now I will answer the question that everyone will soon ask. Why?

"God has been dealing with me about the structuring and the direction of the church, and doing church as usual. God has shown me some powerful things that he would like to be done in this house, but we need to position ourselves. The things that He has commanded us to do as a body of Christ are not being done, at least not at this time. What we done 10 years ago won't work today. We have a different generation of people on our hands. I won't get into it in detail because it is part of the sermon."

"We first need to really understand our positions in the church. What does it really mean to be a deacon or an elder? I believe that we have strayed away from our calling. I am the pastor of this church, and the job requires more than just giving sermons every Saturday. Some of you have a word from God that should be heard. One of the first changes to be made is one of the elders will preach a sermon once every other month. I would also like to have guest speakers come once a quarter to speak. God has a word for the people in this congregation, and plus I need to be ministered to also."

"I would like to see a strong youth program being started soon. We will start elderly services and activities as well. Also our married couples ministry, and singles ministry needs some restructuring."

"First order of business will be some of these new programs will need someone to head them up. I wanted us to come together and get a list of names so we can see if these people will be interested. We might need to change leadership in other ministries. I would like to have a Praise and Worship Ministry to include a youth dance ministry in place for the promotional ceremony. Now I would like to suggest that Sister Sharon Hemphill to head up those groups. Do I have any objection? Deacon Hemphill I wondered if you would ask her if she would be interested. We have approached her about working with the youth, but now it is official in what we would like for her to do."

"Yes sir and she has express delight in you thinking of her, and says that she would be honored to do whatever you needed her to do."

"Great! Now I would like to have light appetizers and drinks after the ceremony. I am requesting the hospitality committee to handle all food services from now on. Does anyone have any suggestions on who should head that up the hospitality committee?"

"I would like to suggest Sister Hemphill. We can all agree that we love her food. She is well organized and everyone loves her."

"Does anyone object to Elder Clark's suggestion?"

"Good I will approach Sister Hemphill on this matter Sunday afternoon after service. Now let's get down to the promotions. Who is being considered to become a deacon? I have met with the elders and we have few candidates for elders."

"Well Pastor as you know Brother Derrick was considered to be a Deacon, but I feel that someone else should handle this one."

"Why is that Deacon?"

"I don't want it to be a conflict of interest, seeing that he was dating my daughter."

"I understand deacon, but I think I speak for everyone in this room when I say that we trust your judgment, and have faith in your decision will be a godly one. Now that you have brought up Brother McCoy what is the status on a decision about his promotion?"

"Well Brother McCoy has been a faithful member for over a year. He has been dedicated in service. I just don't think that he is ready to become a deacon at this time."

"Have you done a background check on Brother McCoy Deacon Hemphill?"

"Yes sir I have. As we all know, I can only discuss my findings with you, and Brother Derrick, but I feel he needs time, and some mentoring before he becomes a deacon."

"Deacon Hemphill, continue to give me a rundown of the rest of the candidates."

"Give me some background on Brother Johnson."

"Brother Johnson has served as head of the men usher board, and he sings in the men choir. Brother Johnson has faithfully served the church for the past three years, and

Deacon Smith has been mentoring Brother Johnson for the past year."

"Is there anyone else?"

"Yes, we have Brother Wilson. Brother Wilson has served in the church for the past five years. He keeps the church clean; make sure fresh flowers are in the church every Sunday. He serves as an usher, and on the building committee. Brother Wilson has been mentored by Deacon Smalls for the past year. We have also considered Brother Scott. Brother Scott has been an active member for the past three years."

"Thank you Deacon Hemphill. I have all their applications and will review them over the next two months. Also let's line up a guest speaker for that day."

"Miranda."

"Yes, Mrs. Edna

"What is the meeting about?"

"I really don't know."

"Miranda I know you know what the meeting is about. You didn't type up an agenda, or anything? You are the

Pastor's secretary I know he told you some of what's going on?"

"You are right about one thing Mrs. Edna, I did type an agenda, but the agenda was not discussed with me. I do the service that is required of me and I don't ask a lot of questions. So I don't know what the meeting is about." Lord this woman is one nosy lady, and she does not give up. I will be glad when we get to her house. Thank God I only have two more exits before I get to the Sugar Creek exit. I never thought it would take this long to get to Hidden Valley. It don't seem to take this long to get to the University area. Must be because I am ready for her to get out of my car.

"Well tell me what is on the agenda then."

"Mrs. Edna why is it so important for you to know what is going on with the meeting?"

"Because I do a lot for this church, and I feel like I have a right to know what is going on. I have invested a lot into this place. I feel like I basically been there since the start."

"Okay, well do you think that you are the only one that has invested into this church? Every one that has tithed into this ministry has invested in it. Others have sacrificed their time and money also, and you don't see them trying to find out every little thing that goes on."

"I don't know if they do, or don't I just know that I have been going here for a long time. I have seen Pastors come and go, and I think if changes are to be made, I have a right to know."

"You are right you do have a right to know, but in the right time. Don't you think the Pastor will announce the changes to everyone when the time is right?"

"I don't know, and don't care. I just don't want to know when the time is right. I want to know right now. I want to know before everyone else. I don't want to find out during an announcement or a business meeting!"

"So what's important to you is not the changes, but knowing something before everyone else? Even if you knew about what is going on in the meeting before everyone else what would you do with the information?"

"What do you mean, what would I do with the information?"

"Like I said, what would you do with the information?"

"I don't know what you are talking about?"

"Okay let me put it a different way and with no disrespect, but who would you run and tell first?"

"Ms. Miranda I don't appreciate what you are trying to say about me."

"And what is it that you think that I am trying to say about you?"

"That I am some busybody or something. You act as if I just do nothing but gossip!"

"Well if the shoe fits……"

"Make a left up here on Tom Hunter Road."

Well at least that shut her up.

"Make a right on Montieth Drive, and I am the fifth house on the right. Thank you Ms. Miranda for taking me home, you have a good night."

"Mrs. Edna, whose gold Mercedes is in your driveway? It seems as though I have seen that car before."

"Mind your own business Ms. Thang." (Bam)

Now, did that old crazy chic just slam my car door!

Chapter 8

This has been one tiresome week. I thought this week would never end. I can't wait to get home to soak in the tub, and read a book. Since I have to stop by K-mart to pick up some toiletries I'll look and see what books they have.

"Hello."

"Good evening sweetheart, how are you doing?"

"Hi daddy, is everything alright?"

"Yes everything is fine, why do you ask?"

"Because you don't call me just to chat, you usually call me when you have something specific to say. You always make it short and sweet, and that's why I love you straight to the point no beating around the bush."

"Okay, well let me get to the point then. I just called to tell you that the Pastor has requested that I ask you if you would like to start a praise and worship dance team at the church. He would also like for you to work with the youth."

"Daddy I would love to!"

"That's good to hear. Now he would like for them to perform at the promotional ceremony."

"Daddy, that's in three months!"

"I know honey. The announcement will be made Sunday for sign up. Sharon are you sure you are going to have time to do this?"

"Yes. How many dances do we get to perform?"

"Well prepare two. Now I can tell you he plans for this to be one powerful, and spirited filled night, so make the dances just like that."

"I will. Daddy how did the Pastor know that I like to dance? Did you tell him?"

"No, but he has been to our home and he probably seen some of your dance recital pictures and some competition trophies. And you know how your mother loves to pull out the photo albums."

"You're right about that. Well thanks again Dad."

"You're welcome sweetheart, and you be careful. Drive home safely."

"I will. Bye Daddy."

Now when I go to K-mart I can check out the music department. I am so excited I can't wait to get started.

K-mart is a little crowded tonight, which is a shocker. That is one reason I drove all the way over to Pineville is because I thought I could get in and get out. Well I am here now so I may as well get my stuff and get out of here. Oh my God! There is Derrick! I wonder if I could just slip down an aisle without him seeing me. No! I'm not running and hiding. It's been over a month since I found out about him and Shelia. I never even called him on it. I left it alone. I pray that he is happy.

"Hi Sharon."

"Hello Derrick, how are you?"

"I'm fine, how about you?"

"I'm fine."

"Sharon I have been thinking a lot about you."

"Oh really, Derrick I don't think we should go there."

"Why not, I was just wondering if you think there is a chance that we could get together and talk?"

"Derrick what is it that we have to talk about? I think that we have said everything that needs to be said."

"Please Sharon. I really need to talk to you; it's a lot I need to explain."

"Derrick I really don't think that is a good idea."

"Oh, Hi Sharon."

"Hello Shelia."

"Derrick honey I'm ready to check out. Did you find everything you need?"

"No I'll pick up my stuff tomorrow."

"Derrick that's silly. We are already here so we may as well get your stuff while we're here."

"You go ahead and check out I will be up there in a minute."

"Derrick, why can't you come with me now?"

"Shelia I said I will be there in a minute."

"Derrick, Shelia both of you have a good night."

"Wait Sharon I needed to talk to you about something. Shelia will you please excuse us?"

"Derrick you see that Sharon is ready to go and I think it's time for us to go."

"Shelia I asked you to excuse us, so could you please go and check out?"

"Derrick what is it that you think you have to say to me. It is now very clear that we have nothing to say to each other."

"Sharon don't say that. I think you are misunderstanding what is going on here. Shelia needed a ride to the store so I gave her one."

"Yeah and I bet she gave you a ride too. Derrick what you do is your business. I don't have to deal with you anymore."

"Sharon you don't have to be like that. I thought you had more class than this."

"I do that's why I am getting ready to walk away. Goodbye Derrick."

"Wait Sharon I want to know if you have thought about me. I mean do you miss us?"

"What does that matter? Obviously, you don't miss us."

"Sharon I do miss us. I miss you. I would like for us to have dinner one more time. Its some things I need to discuss with you. Please Sharon, think about it, and I'll call you next week. I got to go. I'll talk to you later."

Lord I know I am hearing things. This man thinks that I am going out with him. That will be the day. Let me just get the things I came in here for so I can go home.

(Knock, knock, knock)

"Hi Shelia."

"Hey Wanda, can I come in?"

"Sure, come on in. What's going on?"

"Where are the kids?"

"Sharon came over earlier to pick them up. They are going to church with her tomorrow."

"Well you probably already know that I saw your sister at K-mart last night."

"Which sister?"

"Sharon, I figured that she would have already called you and told you that she saw me and Derrick at K-mart."

"My sister doesn't bother with little things like that, but it seems to bother you though. What's wrong with you?"

"Well Derrick and I went to K-mart last night, and when we got into the store we went our separate ways to pick items that we needed. I come back to the front of the store and I see your sister all up in Derrick's face."

"Maybe it's not what it looks like."

"Well the reason I came over here is to ask you to tell Sharon to stay away from Derrick. She had her chance and she couldn't hold on to him. Last night I seen the look in her eyes and it looks like she is trying to get back with him."

"I very seriously doubt it. It was my sister that broke it off with him. So I don't think that she will go back to him. If she wanted Derrick she would still be with him. Why not just ask Derrick what the conversation was all about?"

"Derrick won't talk about her, but if she was taking care of him and handling her business then he wouldn't be with me! You really need to check your sister, always running up in your house like she's miss goody to shoes or something. Grabbing your kids every weekend like they are her kids. If she like kids that much then she should have some of her own."

"Hold on a minute heifer! Now you don't know what my relationship with my sister is like. I really enjoy the time to myself. Don't hate because you have no one to watch your bad ass kids, except yo Momma, and that's only every once in a while."

"I don't need nobody to watch my kids. I can handle my kids, but you must can't if you need your sister to come and get them all the time."

"I don't need no damn body to come and get my kids! Don't hate because my kids are better taken care of because of my family. Hell the only reason you got Derrick is because he wanted sex."

"Well if it's just sex it is damn good sex, because I am the one wearing the ring on my finger. I'm the one he's sleeping with, and I'm the one he says I love you to. Your sister couldn't have him back if she tried."

"Shelia if you really believed that why are you over here bringing this mess to me. See I believe you think I will call my sister and tell her about our conversation, but I would never bother my sister with this nonsense. You are uneasy about seeing Sharon and Derrick together, because if you weren't you wouldn't be over here. You are right about one thing you are wearing the ring on your finger, but it was on my sister's finger first. Now that makes you second choice."

"If Derrick was so into Sharon as you seem to think then why wouldn't he get everything he needed from her? He was with Sharon for show."

"I believe Derrick really wanted Sharon to be his wife, and she might have been for show, but you were only around to be his Ho. Now get the hell out of my house! Bum Bitch Bye!"

"Hello."

"Hey Sharon, this is Derrick."

"What can I do for you?"

"Just wanted to know if we could go out and get something to eat and talk?"

"No, I really don't think that would be a good idea."

"I just wanted to talk about what you have planned for the youth."

"Derrick what is it that you want from me. I will have to work with you in church, but baby don't twist it we will not be interacting outside of church."

"Oh, so it's like that? You're not going to meet me?"

"No. I see no reason for us to meet."

"Okay if you say so, but I want you to know that I will have the last say. I also wanted to let you know that I will call a meeting for all youth leaders, and anyone interested in working with the youth."

"When are you going to call this meeting?"

"It will be next week; an announcement will be made on Sunday."

"Okay."

"Well since you are doing the praise & worship dance. I need to know how many dances, and to what songs."

"You what! Fine Derrick I will email the songs to you tomorrow!"

"Now you know if I don't approve of the songs you will not be able to perform it."

"Whatever! Bye!"

Lord that boy has lost his mind. If I knew Derrick and I had to work together I would have never accepted the position. Lord I am doing this as a service unto you, but this boy here. I really am trying to get him out of my life, and he is determined to be in it.

Chapter 9

"Hello."

"Hi, may I speak to Ms. Hemphill."

"This is she. Who am I speaking with?"

"This is Brian Scott. I approached you at church about my daughter joining the praise and worship dance team."

"How may I help you Mr. Scott?"

"Yes I wanted to know if I could talk to you about my daughter."

"Yes, but Mr. Scott you have only to sign her up. Don't worry I will use every child that will participate."

"I know, but I wanted to discuss a few things with you. I apologize for intruding on your time, but I wouldn't ask if it was not important. As not to inconvenience you more than I already have you tell me when and where we can meet."

"How about tonight, I get off at five o'clock and I could meet you at O Charley's on South Tryon around six thirty. Do you know where that is?"

"Yes I do. I will meet you there."

I don't know what I was thinking about just meeting some strange man I don't even know. What makes matters worse is I am nervous and don't know what to wear. I better hurry and get dress before I am late. I have changed my clothes three times. I have only seen Mr. Scott one time and that's when he approached me in church. I don't know if he is married or not. I was wondering why he approached me and not his wife. Guess my questions should be answered later. I don't want to dress sexy because I don't even know this man. I don't want to dress business casual because I want him to feel comfortable. I should go with some jeans and my cream sweater. This will give me a chance to wear my new cream boots I got from Rack Room Shoes.

I only stay ten or fifteen minutes from O Charley's so it won't take long to get there. All I have to worry about is that Wal-Mart traffic. I will leave now so I can get there early.

I walked into the restaurant, and noticed that Mr. Scott was already there.

"Hello Mr. Scott. How are you?"

"Fine and how are you Ms. Hemphill?"

"I'm fine as usual, but you can call me Sharon."

"Okay Ms. Fine as usual, but only if you call me Brian."

"Well Brian where is your daughter? What is her name again?"

"Her name is Felicia, and I dropped her off at her grandmothers."

"Okay, what did you want to talk to me about?"

"Straight to the point, I like that. Let's order first so we won't be interrupted that much while we are talking."

As he called over the waiter and ordered our food it gave me time to check him out. He is a good looking brother. I love his smile and his white teeth. I like how he took control and set the tone of the evening. You can tell he is a strong man, and that he is used to handling his business. There seems to be no beating around the bush for him.

"Now that the ordering is done let me get to the point. My daughter is a wonderful dancer. Her mother had her taking jazz, ballet, and tap, but ever since her mother died I have not been able to get her to dance. She barely even listens to music or watch videos on TV."

"Have you ever thought that she might not be interested in dancing anymore? The loss of a parent is hard and her way of dealing with it maybe to not dance. It may remind her of her mother, and she can't deal with that right now."

"Yes, I have thought about that, but you didn't see the way she use to light up whenever she was dancing. Whether it was dancing at home or on stage you could tell she really enjoyed it."

"What is it that you want from me Brian? Hold on a minute while I answer this call. Please excuse me."

"Hello this is Sharon speaking how may I help you?"

"Hey baby, what are you doing?"

"I am out to dinner who is this?"

"What do you mean who is this? This is Derrick, who else would it be? Did you say you were out to dinner?"

"Yes I did. What can I do for you?"

"Who are you out with?"

"That's none of your business, and don't call me no more."

"I'm sorry about that Brian go ahead and finishing telling me how I can help you?"

"I was hoping that you can talk to her and get her interested in dancing again. I feel there is a void in her eyes and in her life. I feel like there is a place in her I just can't reach. I know it is a lot to ask of someone who doesn't know me, but I ask that you just pray about it, and whatever you decide I will respect. Honestly this is not your problem, but I just didn't know what else to do or who I could talk to."

"Why did you choose me?"

"I don't know. When I walked up to you in church last week, and you looked up at me and smiled and handed me the form I just felt like I could talk to you."

"Thanks I think. I don't know if there is anything that I can do or say, but I will try and do whatever I can. If you don't mind me asking how did your wife die?"

"She was killed in a car accident by a drunk driver."

"How long has it been?"

"It has been a little over two years now."

"I am so sorry for your loss. How old was your daughter when your wife died?"

"She had just turned eight years old."

As I am sitting here listening to this man's story my heart really goes out to him. There are so many questions I would like to ask him. Sitting here across from him watching him as he eat, wondering how old he was, if he was seeing someone. He moves with so much grace. When he looks up at me his dark eyes look like they can see straight thru to my soul.

"Sharon, I hope I am not being to forward, but are you seeing anyone right now?"

"No not right now, but I was seeing someone."

"May I ask what happened?"

"It just wasn't working out for me. I just can't be with someone that does not want to share their past history with me. I believe if I am going to be with someone I should know a little more about them. I don't want to be with a man that don't want to share his life with me. I want a man that is willing to share the good and the bad, his past as well as his future. I guess that's too much to ask for."

"No it's not. Believe it or not men are looking for the same thing. We want a woman we can share our goals, our future plans with also. It is hard to find women that will listen as well as encourage us, and inspire us to out potential greatness."

"Well Mr. Scott what are your goals, your hopes, and dreams? If I am getting to personal just let me know."

"No it's alright I feel comfortable talking to you. I would love to share my goals with you. My first goal is to be debt free. That includes having my daughters' full college tuition already when that time comes. I want my money to work for me not me having to work for my money. I would like to get married again. I would like to have more children, and I want to buy a few more houses."

"That sounds good, what are your spiritual goals?"

"Well right now I am just an open vessel, and wherever God leads me I will follow."

"Look at the time. I can't believe that it is 10:00 already."

"I do apologize that I let time get away from me like that, I shouldn't have kept you out so long."

"It's alright, it's Friday. It's not like I have anything else to do tomorrow, but I have to be going."

"Okay, let me walk you to your car."

This man is truly a gentleman. He helped me with my coat, walked me to my car, and stood there and talked while my car warmed up. I tried to get him to sit in my car so he wouldn't have to stand in the cold, but he said he was fine. He gave me his card with his number on it so I could call him when I got home. He just wants to know that I got home safely. That is so sweet of him. I loved sitting there listening to him talk he has such a smooth and sexy voice.

His voice is smooth like Barry White, but not as deep. It's like a perfect tenor tone. Glad I left lights on in the house, even though I was not expecting to get back this late. I barely get in the door and the phone is already ringing.

"Hello."

"Oh, so you finally decided to come home from your date!"

"How do you know I just got home?"

"Don't worry about how I know. Where have you been?"

"I must be hearing things, cause I know you didn't just ask me where I been? I don't owe you any explanations of where I go or who I go out with! Now I have asked you not to call me anymore. If you would like to discuss church issues then we will discuss them at church."

"You know that you and I are supposed to be together. I don't know why you are playing around. Just because you gave me back the ring doesn't mean that we are not still with each other, it just means that you are not ready to get married right now."

"Boy, are you crazy? When I gave you back that ring it meant I do not want to see you anymore."

"Well that's not the way I took it."

"Considering that you were seeing me and Shelia at the same time is definitely another reason we are finished."

"I tried to tell you that Shelia was just a friend. There is nothing going on between her and I. she is a single mother having a hard time and I was just helping her out. The bible says we are supposed to help the fatherless."

"That Is Funny To Me! I guess with all the help you were giving her you had to help her in and out of bed. And it must have been good to you so you had to put a ring on her finger."

"That was just a friendship ring. It means nothing."

"Must mean something it was an engagement ring for me. It doesn't matter the bottom line is that we are no longer together. You may see whoever you want to see, and I can do the same."

"Look I am not giving up on us. God meant for us to be together, and I promise you we will be together."

"Whatever Derrick, get off my phone."

Lord is that man crazy! Let me call Brian before he thinks that I have forgotten about him.

"Hello."

"Hi Brian, just wanted to let you know I got home safely."

"Girl I was getting ready to send out an APB on you."

"Why?"

"Well you told me that you didn't stay far, and it was taking you a long time to call me back. I was getting worried."

"That's sweet of you to worry about me, even though you don't know me."

"I would like to get to know you if that is alright with you."

"I tell you what, how about you and Felicia come over to my Mom's house for dinner on Sunday?"

"Sure, but does your Mom know that I am coming?"

"Not yet, but she doesn't mind. She loves having company over. I will bring my nephew and niece over so Felicia will have someone there her age."

"Okay I will get the address from you on Sunday."

"I will see you Sunday, and thanks again for dinner."

"No problem, it's the least I could do considering that you sat and listen to my problems. Sleep well."

I don't know what made me invite him over to my parent's house for dinner. Now I have to call Mom and let her know. I had already planned to pick up T and T this weekend so we can go to church and hang out. Tawanda wants to join the dance team, and I have practice tomorrow at the center on Tuckaseegee Rd. That was the only place that would allow me to have practice without charging me.

"Hi Wanda, Hi Sharon."
"Hey Sis, the kids will be out in a minute, have a seat."
"Thanks."
"So Sis how is it going?"
"Fine."
"Okay let's get to the point. What's up with the fine brother that was over Mom's house Sunday?"
"Oh you mean Brian?"
"Yes I mean Brian! Is that your new man?"
"No we are just friends. He is just interested in his daughter joining the dance team at church."
"No sweetie, that's not all he is interested in."
"How do you know that Wanda?"
"Girl the way he was looking at you. You would think that man was in love."
"Wanda quit it. You know that is not true."
"Trust me yes…it is. How long have you known him?"

"We met a month ago."

"Well he looked like he was right at home at Mom's house."

"He has been over for dinner a few times."

"Dad seems to really like him. If I had not gone to the back room to speak to Dad I would have never seen him."

"Yeah, he and Dad seem to click right away."

"So what are you going to do?"

"What do you mean?"

"Are you going to hook up with him or what?"

"All I can say is that we are just friends."

"Well they say friends make the best lovers."

"That's what they say, but we shall see."

"We're ready Aunt Sharon! Where are we going?"

"Well Tawanda and I have dance practice and after that we will be heading off to the movies."

"Can I call Felicia and see if she wants to come?"

"Yes, but I think that she will be at dance practice."

"Hey Sharon."

"Hello Derrick, how can I help you?"

"Are you seeing somebody?"

"What business is it of yours?"

"Because you were just seeing me and now you are seeing someone else. Do you know how that makes you look?"

"First of all I am not seeing anyone, and I really don't care how it looks to everyone."

"If, you're not seeing anyone then who is Brian, is he the tall dark skinned negro with the wavy hair?"

"Yes he is, Brian is just a friend and his daughter comes to dance practice. Look, like I told you before I don't owe you any explanation and I will not stand out here discussing this with you!"

"Well maybe I need to sit in on your practice today so I can see what's going on."

"Whatever Derrick, I got to go inside to start practice."

Lord I can't believe Derrick showed up at my rehearsal. I wonder what he is up to. I don't know why he can't get it through his thick skull I am not interested in him. I don't like the way he called Brian that darked-skinned brother like he is better because he is light-skinned. I know he might not have meant it like that, but it sure sounded like it.

"Hey man, how's it going?"

"Fine, how about you?"

"I'm alright, by the way my name is Derrick what's yours?"

"My name is Brian; it's nice to meet you."

"Which one of these angels is yours?"

"That's my beautiful daughter Felicia over there standing against the wall. Which one is yours?"

"I don't have any children. I am over the youth ministries, and I am here just to observe, and to see my lady."

"Which one is your lady?"

"The dance teacher."

"Oh really, didn't think that she was seeing anyone."

"What would give you that idea?"

"For one she told me that she was not seeing anyone, and she never talks about a man in her life."

"I don't know why she said that, maybe she was joking with you. Regardless she does have a man, and that man is ME, so if you had any ideas don't even think about."

"I think that is for Sharon to say and not you. Now if you will excuse me!"

Okay I don't like the way this is looking over there. Brian looks like he is upset, and Derrick looks to sneaky for me.

"Felicia, can you come here for a minute please?"

"Yes, Ms. Sharon."

"Felicia I know you said that you don't want to dance, but you have been to all the practices so I know that you are familiar with the routines."

"Yes, but I don't want to dance."

"I understand I just want you to watch the class for me while I step out of the room for a minute. Watch the way they are doing the routine and their moves, and correct them if they are wrong. Just need for you to make sure that they are in the right direction. Do you think you can do that for me?"

"Yes ma'am."

"Thanks sweetheart. I will be right outside the door. Class I have to step out of a minute. Felicia is going to go through the routine with you. If anyone acts up or get out of hand I will sit you down. Okay Felicia please prepare the music and start the routine."

I asked one of the parents to keep an eye out on the class while I step out for a minute. Lord I hope that Derrick has not said anything stupid. Brian looked aggravated when he left out.

"Hey Brian what's going on? Are you alright?"

"Yeah, just needed to get some fresh air it was getting a little stuffy in there."

"Okay what did Derrick say?"

"Just wanted to let me know that you were his lady and for me to not even think about you. Don't worry about it though, because I told him it was your decision. Is this the guy that you were telling me about?"

"Yes it was."

"You didn't tell me it was Brother Derrick."

"I'm sorry didn't think it mattered. I am so sorry Brian about what he said to you, and I appreciate what you said. Just so you know I am not seeing him and I am not his lady."

"Hey baby there you are. What are you doing after practice?"

"Well the children and I are going to the movies with Brian and Felicia."

I hope Brian doesn't mind me throwing him into this mess. I hope he forgives me.

"Sweetheart did you decide on what movie we are going to see?"

"Not yet I figured that we would let the children decide."

"Oh so ya'll trying to play the happy family, and play me like I am a fool! Well, you will soon see you have messed with the wrong brother!"

"My God Derrick it is not that serious. We are not seeing each other anymore. You are seeing Shelia, and you trying to prevent me from seeing someone?"

"Look here Sharon you can't…."

"Whoa, whoa partner I know you didn't just grab my girl's arm like that!"

"It's alright Brian, this conversation is over, and I am going back to my class."

"Oh you best believe this conversation is not over. Not by a long shot, and we will see how long you have your little class!"

"Sharon are you alright?"

"Yes I'm fine. I apologize for putting you in the middle of this."

"It's alright. It was fun at first, until he started tripping."

"I can't believe that Derrick acted like that. He didn't pay me this much attention when we were together."

"Well his loss. You know what they say you never know what you got until it's gone."

"I guess, I don't believe he is really interested in me. I believe he didn't want me until he thought that someone else did. Now if he really knew the truth that no one is interested me then he wouldn't act like that. You know some of us only want what someone else has."

"What do you mean no one is interested in you? I am interested in you."

"Since when?"

"Since the first time that we met at O'Charleys."

"You never said anything! Wait before you comment let me check in on the class and see how Felicia is doing." Whew that was a close call. I was not ready for this conversation. Oh my goodness Felicia is doing a great job; she is even doing the routine with them. Brian was right she lights up and glows when performing. Now how can I get her to perform? I'll just pray about it and let God do His thing. Something good came out of Derrick coming over here acting crazy.

Chapter 10

(Ring, ring)

"Hello."

"Hi Sharon are you busy?"

"No, I am just sitting here watching CSI Miami. Is everything alright Brian?

"Yes, everything is fine just needed to talk to you."

"Okay let me turn off the TV. Go ahead what's on your mind?"

"You are Sharon."

"Okayyyy. Brian did I do or say something to upset you?"

"No it's nothing like that. I just wanted to get back to our previous conversation we were having Saturday afternoon."

"Okay I'm listening."

"I just wanted to reiterate that I am interested in you, and I have been since I first met you. I did not come straight out and say it, but I thought you knew."

"I am sorry Brian I didn't know. I knew that I liked you, but I didn't want to push. You just lost your wife two years ago, and I just didn't know if you were ready. I thought friendship was all you wanted and needed right now."

"I feel that I am ready, but I still have Felicia to consider. How she will feel about me dating is very important. I don't want her to think that I am trying to replace her mother."

"I understand. I am fine with the way things are. You and Felicia both have to be ready."

"Sharon, I am ready now, but I do want to take things slow, so we will have a chance to really get to know each other. Now that I have said all that will you go out with me Friday night?"

"You are so silly, of course I will. Where are we going?"

"I don't know I was going to ask you to pick a place."

"Okay, but are you sure you want me to pick the place?"

"Wait a minute you are scaring me, what do you mean am I sure? Yes I am sure. Wherever you want to go is fine with me. As long as I can be with you it is fine."

"You are so sweet."

"Yeah you say that now. I will let you get back to your show. I will see you on Friday around 7:30."

"Okay, bye."

(Ring, ring)

"Did you forget to tell me something?"

"Yeah, I forgot to tell you that I don't want you seeing that Negro again."

"What? Derrick are you crazy? You can't tell me who to see! I may see whomever I want. NOW DON'T CALL ME AGAIN!!!"

(ring, ring)

"Hello!"

"Sharon we were supposed to be married. Let me correct that we will be married."

"Derrick no….we are not. Why don't you leave me alone? You are seeing Shelia just go be with her and leave me alone."

"Shelia was just a lay. I am planning on marrying you."

"Noooo…you are not. There is no chance in hell I would marry you!"

"We shall see, after I get thru destroying your reputation no man will want you not even Jesus himself!"

"So you have sunk so low as to start threatening me?"

"That's not a threat baby that is a promise."

"Listen Derrick let's just part ways. You don't bother me and I won't bother you. Please don't call me anymore."

Oh my goodness! I don't know what I will do about Derrick, he sounds serious. He might take the hint and leave me alone.

"Hey Laura."

"Hello Edna. How are you?"

"You haven't invited me over for dinner in a while."

"Yes, I know I have been a little busy getting ready for this promotional ceremony."

"Yes, and you didn't call me and asked for my help."

"Right now I have all the people I need on the committee, but if I need any additional assistance I will let you know."

"Well thanks, but that's not the only reason for my call. Wanted to know how you allow your daughter to just sleep around in the church, and your husband is supposed to be a deacon."

"Edna I don't know what you are talking about, nor do I want to know. I don't meddle too much in my children's life."

"That's the problem right there. If you took the time to meddle just a little bit then your children wouldn't be the way they are."

"Look Edna we have raised our children to the best of our ability that God gave us. Now once they are older they are at the age where they are accountable for their own action. I am sure that Sharon is not doing anything to bring shame on herself or our family."

"Well what do you call jumping from one man to another? First she was seeing Brother Derrick, and now she is seeing Brother Brian. Brother Derrick is hurt over this situation."

"Oh really and how do you know?"

"I just do."

"I haven't talked to Sharon about it. If she feels like talking about it she will call me."

"Well I'm just saying that it doesn't look good for her to be sleeping around in the church. How does that look to the young'uns? She is setting a bad example."

"Hold on a minute Edna. Sharon would do nothing to set a bad example for children. Sharon really love children and that was one reason I believe that she was chosen for that position."

"Yeah right, she got that position because she is yawls daughter!"

"You know what Edna; I have entertained you long enough. I am getting off the phone."

"You don't have to discuss it with me, but I will be meeting with the Pastor next week and I will be discussing it with him. Just thought I would let you know."

"Bye Edna."

"Brad, can you come here a moment?"

"What is it honey?"

"I just got off the phone with Edna."

"Oh Lord, what did she say now?"

"She claims that Sharon is sleeping around in the church!"

"What? Where is she getting this mess?"

"I don't know. I know Sharon stop seeing Derrick, but I don't know anyone else that she is seeing."

"Laura, why do you let that woman get to you?"

"I'm afraid that she is going to do something hurtful with her gossiping. She says that she has a meeting with the Pastor next week and she will tell him that Sharon shouldn't be working with the youth. She feels that Sharon is setting a bad example for the children."

"Laura don't worry God will work it out."

"Miranda do I have any other appointments other than Sister Edna?"

"No sir, I made sure not to schedule anything else."

"Thank you Miranda, and could you call Deacon Hemphill and ask him if he could come to this meeting if he is free."

(Knock, knock)

"Come in."

"Good afternoon Pastor."

"Good afternoon Sister Edna."

"I have brought Brother Derrick with me."

"Not that I mind, but May I ask why?"

"Because he has witness some of the things that I want to talk to you about."

"I see, alright well we will start in a minute just waiting on Deacon Hemphill, oh here he comes."

"Why is he here?"

"I always have a Deacon or Elder present when I have a counseling session. Miranda will also sit in due to the fact that you are a woman. We make sure that we have another woman present when counseling a woman. Brother Derrick can you give a word of prayer and I will pray after you, then we will get into the meeting."

"Let's bow our head. Dear Heavenly Father we thank you again for your grace and mercy which endureth forever. Lord we come before you with heavy hearts. You know the issues that we face, and we pray today that everything can be resolved. We will be so careful to give you all the praise honor and glory. In Jesus name Amen."

"Now I will give a word of prayer."

"Dear God our Lord and Savior we come before you today as humble servants, trying to do your will, not our will. We ask that you continue to work through our imperfections to prefect your works. Help us to be an example to each other and to those out in the world. Please send the Holy Spirit down to dwell with us in this meeting. Lord please, please guide and direct this meeting how it should go. We give this prayer in Jesus name Amen."

"Now Sister Edna we will start with you since you requested this meeting. You have concerns about the direction the ministry is taking."

"Yes, first of all you never addressed the congregation to ask how we feel about the changes."

"Let me say this. This church does not belong to you or me. It is God's house and since God has sent me here to shepherd His flock then it is my job to guide the sheep in the direction that God has directed me to, and our feelings really don't matter."

"I disagree, I think some of our feelings do matter considering some of us have been here a long time and have time, and money invested in the success of this church."

"Yes, and Jesus has a lot invested in us, and we cannot begin to be able to give Him a return on his investment. He paid it all for us, and we yet whine and complain. Just remember sister this is just a building until we all assemble here. We bring church with us."

"Pastor I still feel that some of us should be consulted about the changes that are being made."

"Okay I understand that you feel that you should be consulted, but that is not the way that I am running this church. Some of the changes being made are being brought before the church board, and then church business meetings."

"I used to know everything that went on at church now I seem to be kept in the dark about everything. This is done on purpose. Deacon Hemphill could testify to that."

"No I cannot. I can't speak on anything that I know nothing about."

"You know that I haven't been to your house for dinner. Sister Laura doesn't call me on the phone to check up on me like she used to."

"Don't take it personally. My wife has been very busy lately, more than usual. I really do not wish to discuss my wife. If her name comes up she should be here to speak for herself."

"That's correct Deacon Hemphill. We will discuss no one in this meeting that's not here to speak for themselves. Sister Edna all I keep hearing is about you. You know this ministry does not revolve around you, me, or anyone else but Jesus Christ."

"Should have known that you were going to say that, and I knew when Deacon Hemphill showed up how this meeting was going to go. I knew that you would try to protect your daughter. She probably told you some lies and that's why you want to be in this meeting."

"Sister Edna you are out of order! Deacon Hemphill was just called this morning and asked if he could attend this meeting. He had no idea I was meeting you before today. Now if you wanted to discuss Sister Sharon then we need to post pone this meeting until such a time she can attend."

"Well Pastor I did know that you were meeting with Sister Edna. She called my wife and told her. So when you called me and asked me to attend I thought it would be best."

"Is this true Sister Edna?"

"Yes it is. I felt she had a right to know what was going on with her daughter. I don't think this can wait any longer. You have someone working with the youth setting a bad example."

"Again Sister Edna if you are talking about anyone other than the people in this room then we are unable to discuss it."

"So you are fine with Sharon sleeping around in the church and working with the youth. What is that teaching our young people? They have enough things poisoning their minds, and now we are poisoning their mind in the church. You need to sit her down until she gets herself together. Now she had a good man when she was with Brother Derrick here, but she has gotten tired of him, and now she is with Brother Brian, taking advantage of that poor man. You know he lost his wife only two years ago."

"Now wait a minute, I have heard enough…."

"Hold on Deacon Hemphill I think it is time we end this meeting with pray. We will schedule another meeting with Sister Sharon and Brother Brian present."

"Why? I think you just need to sit her little behind down now or else!"

"Now is a good time for us to pray and go home. But first when would you like to have the next meeting?"

"I don't want another meeting. As the Pastor of this church I need for you to do your job."

"I tell you what Sister Edna there is a board meeting next Monday night. You can voice your grievance in front of the board and Sister Sharon since it is her character being attacked."

"No I will not. I presented my grievances to you, but I see you will not do what needs to be done. God will take of it watch and see."

"Your right Sister Edna, God will take care of it. Okay now let's pray."

"Ya'll go ahead and pray I am leaving. Come on Derrick let's go."

"Deacon Hemphill, Sister Miranda I would appreciate if things said in this room not be repeated. Deacon I know you will want to sit down and talk with Sister Sharon, but please be cautious. We do not want this thing to get out of hand. Let's not give the devil any more ammunition than he already has. God will get the glory out of this and it will work itself out. Now let's pray."

Chapter 11

"Hey Dad."

"Hey baby."

"Why did you call me over here?"

"Your Mother and I need to talk to you."

"What's wrong?"

"Well the other day the Pastor called me to the church for a meeting. When I got there Sister Edna and Derrick was there. She wanted the Pastor to sit you down from working with the youth. She says that you are setting the wrong example for the youth."

"What? How am I setting the wrong example?"

"She claims that you are sleeping around in the church."

"Dad that is a lie, and what did Derrick have to say?"

"He didn't say anything. Edna did all the talking."

"This must be what Derrick meant when he said that he would ruin my reputation and that nobody would want me."

"Sharon why didn't you tell me that Derrick was threatening you?"

"Because Mom I thought he was just talking. I never thought he would drag my name through the mud."

"Don't worry about it honey just keep doing what you are doing with the youth. Everything will work itself out.

"The Pastor might call another meeting with you present. If Edna continues to make this an issue he will have no choice, but to call a meeting."

"I am ready. I would love to be in a meeting with Mrs. Edna and Derrick. I am ready for a meeting now!"

"Sweetheart can I ask you a question?"

"Sure Mom, what is it?"

"What is going on between you and Brian?"

"We are just friends right now. We went out a couple of times. I am not going to lie to you I really like Brian a lot."

"So what are you planning to do? Are you going to start seeing him? Are you dating now?"

"I don't know. He wants to take it slow because of Felicia, and I agreed. I would never want to traumatize a child so I can wait to see where this takes us."

"So is Derrick jealous or what?"

"It's more like or what. I don't know what is up with him. When I broke it off with him he seemed fine. He was seeing someone else while he was seeing me. It wasn't until he thought I was seeing someone else that he tripped."

"Mom, Dad I don't know what to do?"

"It's alright honey everything is going to work out you'll see. I tell you what baby let me handle it."

"Okay dad. I am going home."

"Call us as soon as you get home."

Lord I don't understand what Mrs. Edna has against me. I have done nothing to her. I never thought Derrick would go to such extremes. I need to call Brian. I hope he is home.

"Hello."

"Hi Brian, are you busy?"

"No. I am never too busy for you. What's up?"

"My dad just told me that they had a meeting the other day with the Pastor, and Mrs. Edna has requested that he sit me down from working with the youth. She says that I am setting a bad example. Derrick was also there."

"Calm down Sharon, now how do they think that you are setting a bad example?"

"They say I am sleeping around the church, first with Derrick and now with you. Derrick and I have never had sex the whole time we were dating!"

"Why do you think they are doing this?"

"I don't know why Mrs. Edna is doing this, but I know why Derrick is doing this."

"Do you want to come over for a little bit?"

"No that's alright, but I appreciate you asking. I am going to just go home and take a long hot bath."

"Are you sure? We don't mind you coming over. I talked with Felicia and she really enjoys having you around."

"Apologize to Felicia for me, but I think I will just go home. I will talk to you tomorrow."

"Okay if you are sure. Call me and let me know that you got home safely. If you need to talk call me anytime."

I wish I could just go over to Brian's house and relax, but this thing has got me bothered, and I wouldn't be good company. I miss him and Felicia. He is such a good man. I can't believe that he likes me the way that he does. He is a good listener and very attentive. The thing I love the most is he is such a great father. I love to see men take care of their children. Now that is a turn on for me.

"Hello."

"Sharon."

"Yes. Who is this?"

"It's me, Derrick."

"Derrick what do you want? Do you realize that it is 3:00 in the morning?"

"Yes, and I am so sorry that I called you this early, but I have been thinking about things and I need to talk to you."

"Derrick I was sleep. I can't talk right now, can't this wait until later?"

"Sharon please I just want to say that I am sorry about what happened between us."

"What about what happened in the meeting with the Pastor?"

"Oh, so you heard about that already? I apologize for that to, but you got to know that I didn't say anything against you."

"Okay Derrick I accept your apology. Now I got to go to sleep."

"Can I ask you one more question?"

"What is it?"

"Do you think that we can be friends?"

"Maybe, now I got to go."

"Church I would like to make an announcement. We are moving the promotional ceremony to later in the year. I do apologize for any inconvenience, but I think it is necessary to make those changes. We will enter the New Year with a new board, and some people moving to the next level in God. In all fairness I was rushing it a little and I apologize. To be fair I want to give everyone enough time to get everything completed for this special occasion. I am looking forward to this blessed event.

(Ring, ring)

"Hello."

"Derrick, have you heard from Pastor Brown about your deacon position?"

"No not yet, but he did call and request a meeting for next week."

"What about Sharon? Have you decided to move on? You know you can do better?"

"Yeah I guess, but you have to admit that we would have made an awesome couple in the church. We could have made a powerful couple in the church. Becoming a deacon was only the beginning."

"Well it's her loss. Now she has to settle for being with a regular Joe with no spiritual aspiration except to be an usher. That man has been an usher for the past 3 years."

"That's what she wanted; now she will just have to deal with it."

"You know you will have to be careful of who you choose for a wife now. I can tell you one thing, that hood rat you are seeing is not deacon wife material."

"Yes I know. I will be given her the boot as soon as it is confirmed that I get the position. Have you noticed any other prospects in the church?"

"Yes it is a couple of young ladies that would make a nice wife for you. They are not a perfect fit as Sharon, but they will do."

"I'll call you after the meeting with the Pastor."

"Okay, but I will see you later right?"

"Probably not I will be getting home late. I will call you tomorrow from work to check on you."

(Ring, ring)

"Hello."

"Hi Sharon."

"Hello Derrick what can I do for you?"

"Nothing, just called to see how you were doing."

"I am fine as usual, how about you?"

"I am doing alright. How are you and Brian doing?"

"Derrick I said maybe we could be friends. I will not discuss Brian and our relationship with you, because it is none of your business."

"Okay I apologize. I hope things are going well for the two of you."

"Thanks."

"I just called to see how you were doing. I guess I will talk to you later."

"Goodbye Derrick."

I don't know about Derrick and I being friends, but I guess I can be cordial to him since he is trying. I was surprise he asked about Brian considering how he acted a month ago. If he knew how I felt about Brian now he would flip. The feelings I have for Brian are nothing like the feelings I had for Derrick. I believe that I was trying to force myself to have feelings for Derrick. The feelings I had were more of a friendship feeling. I am falling in love with Brian, and Felicia is my heart. I love that little girl. Derrick really sounded good. I am glad he got over whatever issues he was having with me.

"Pastor Brown, Brother Derrick McCoy is here for his appointment."
"Thanks Miranda, please show him in."
"Good evening Brother Derrick. You know Elder Clark. We are going to start off with a word of prayer."
"Dear Heavenly Father we thank you for this time of gathering. We invite you to be in the mist of this meeting. Father we ask that you guide this meeting in the way that you desire for it to go. We ask Lord for a special out pouring of your Spirit in this place. We ask this in Jesus name Amen."
"Brother Derrick as you know you were recommended as a candidate for a deacon position. After prayerful consideration was done it was decided that another year of mentoring would be beneficial before being appointed a deacon."

"What part of the process was not satisfactory that you all would feel that I was not ready now?"

"It's not a particular part of the process that was not satisfactory. We would just be doing you an injustice. If you are put in a position you are not spiritually ready for. It could damage you and the church."

"I understand that, but what gave you the impression that I was not spiritually ready for this responsibility. Was there something said or done to make you believe that I was not ready?"

"No, I would just like to see you a little more involved, and that was one of the reasons why I asked you to be a part of the youth ministry. Also you have only been here a little over a year and we don't know that much about you. We therefore decided that another year of mentoring before being appointed was needed."

"So you decided not to add me to the deacon board?"

"That's correct I just don't feel like you are spiritually at a point where you are ready to take the on the responsibility of a deacon."

"So, you are really saying that you want to try and humble me by seeing me serve in a menial position."

No, basically we would just like to get to know you better spiritually, physically, and mentally."

"So you have appointed others? May I ask who you decided on?"

"No, it would not be appropriate to discuss that with you. The other parties don't know yet. It really doesn't matter; it did not affect the decision one way or another."

"What about Deacon Hemphill?"

"What about him?"

"Did he affect the decision one way or another?"

"I will not discuss Deacon Hemphill with you, but I can say that I respect the opinion of my deacons and elders. It was voted on and the decision has been made."

"Okay, well thank you Pastor for taking the time to personally speak to me."

"No problem Brother Derrick and it is going to be a pleasure serving with you. I am expecting great and wonderful things from the youth ministry."

"Hello."

"They didn't give me the deacon position. Pastor Brown wants me to continue to serve with the youth ministry."

"What!"

"Yeah, that's what I was thinking. I asked him who did they give the position to, but of course you know he didn't tell me."

"I will find out and call you back or are you coming home?"

"No not right now I have a few stops to make."

They didn't give me the position because of Deacon Hemphill. Now if I was his son-in-law he wouldn't have had a problem putting me in that position. When I become his son-in-law he will change his mind. I just have to convince Sharon we are meant to be together. I need to get Brian out of the picture.

"Hello."

"Hi Sharon."

"Hello Derrick, how are you?"

"Fine as usual as you would say."

"You are funny. What's going on?"

"Just got some bad news, and I really just needed to talk."

"Well I only got a few minutes because Brian will be here in a minute to pick me up. What's going on?"

"Never mind then I will just talk to you later."

"Okay well I hope everything works out for you."

"Oh it will. I promise you it will."

"Hello Elder Clark this is Edna how are you?"

"I am fine Sister Edna, how can I help you?"

"You can help me, by telling me what happened to Derrick becoming a deacon? You practically guaranteed that he would get the position!"

"No Edna I told you that I would recommend him and it would be a good chance. I fought hard for him and he did get my vote."

"So whose vote didn't he get other than Deacon Hemphill?"

"I can't tell you that Edna."

"Oh really, so do you want me to tell your wife what I know."

"No Edna. He didn't get that many votes. People don't really know him."

"And whose fault is that? It was your job for them to know more about him. Church is like politics you have to lobby for things you want. Now who got the position?"

"Brother Brian Scott got one of the positions and the other one went to…"

"Wait a minute! I didn't just hear you say Brian Scott the one seeing Sharon Hemphill!"

"Yes. He has been here awhile, and he is a faithful tither, and a faithful servant."

"Why are you singing his praises? You act as though you would rather see him in the position instead of Derrick."

"It is not that Edna, it is just that we have known Brother Brian longer. He was unanimously voted in. I thought that both of them would get a position."

"Well what are you going to do about it?"

"Edna there is nothing I can do. It has already been voted on and the decision is made."

"We will see about that!"

"Edna don't make things worse. What is done is done. He will get his chance I promise."

"Your promises mean nothing to me anymore Clark."

"Edna please!"

"Goodbye!"

"Hey Derrick I found out who got one of the deacon positions."

"Who was it?"

"Brian."

"Brian who, and please don't tell me the one that Sharon is dating."

"Yes, that's the one!"

"How the hell did he get the position? So the perfect little couple think that they can make a fool out of me! Well I will show them, you wait and see!"

"Calm down Derrick, we will take care of this. Just be patient."

"No, I am going to take care of this real soon."

"What are you going to do?"

"Don't worry about it, I got this. I am going to handle things my way from now on."

"Derrick I don't like the way you are sounding. Please come home so we can talk about this."

"I'll be home in a little while, don't worry. Give me about an hour."

"Okay"

(Knock, knock, knock)

"Who is it?"

"Shelia it's me Derrick."

"Hey baby I haven't heard from you. I have been calling you and you are not returning my calls. Is everything alright?"

"Yeah, I just stopped by to tell you something."

"What's going on?"

"Sharon and I got back together and we decided to get married this weekend."

"What? You're kidding right? You have to be kidding. You have been spending all your time with me up until last week and you are now telling me that you are going to marry that heifer! Hell to the nah! How long has it been since you two started back seeing each other? I bet she don't know that you were still sleeping with me. I think I need to tell her."

"No you won't be telling her anything. Now I will let go of your neck, and I want you to remember how close you came to me choking you to death if you even think about talking to Sharon or anyone else. I have no problem returning and slapping the taste out of your mouth again. Do you understand me?"

"Yes Derrick."

"Now go and pack anything that is mine and put it in the suitcase that I brought over here. I want you to know that you were the best lay I have ever had. Oh yeah take off Sharon's ring!"

Chapter 12

I am so glad this day is almost over!! Lord if this phone rings one more time! OMG!!!!!!

"Hello."

"Sharon! Terells' school bus was in a bad accident and he has been rushed to the hospital!"

"Oh my God! Derrick how do you know?"

"I was at Shelia's house packing my things when Shelia got a call from your sister."

"Thanks Derrick I got to go. I need to call Wanda and my Mom. I need to find out what hospital. Why didn't anyone call me?"

"It just happened they will probably call. They took him to Carolinas Medical Center. I am right downstairs parked in front of the building. Just run on down and I can take you to the hospital. We can make it over there in 5 to 10 minutes. You can get Brian to bring you back over to get your car."

"I am on my way."

"Derrick I would like to thank you again. I am a nervous wreck."

"It's okay. I know how much you love your nephew, and I knew you wouldn't be in any condition to drive."

"You're right, but I do need to call Mom."

"She's probably already at the hospital and you know that there is no reception in there. You will see her in a minute."

"Well I am going to try and call anyway."

"Hello Mom, are you at the hospital yet?"

"Sharon, why would I be at the hospital?"

"Because Terells' school bus had a really bad accident and he was rushed to the hospital."

"Sharon, Terell and Tawanda are in the den playing with your father. What would make you think he was in the hospital? Hello Sharon! Hello! Hello Sharon!"

"Derrick what's going on? Why did you snatch my phone from me? Why did you tell me that Terell was in an accident?"

"Sharon calm down. I tried to tell you not to call your Mom. Sorry I lied, but you wouldn't come down unless it was something drastic."

"Derrick, why are you doing this? Why are you getting on the highway? Where are you going?"

"We are going home."

"Home where Derrick? I don't understand!"

"You always want to know where I live. You kept bugging me about my house. Well I am taking you to my house."

"Derrick you are scaring me, please take me home."

"I am taking you home. If you will be my wife then my home is your home."

"Derrick I am not going to be your wife. I am seeing Brian now."

"That was only temporary. I told him you were my girl."

"Derrick how can I get you to understand that there is no chance for us. We had our chance and it just wasn't meant to be."

"Sharon how come you can't seem to forgive me? You don't believe in second chances. I know Shelia was a mistake, but I regret it and I am asking for your forgiveness."

"Derrick you don't need my forgiveness what's done is done. I have no hard feelings towards you or Shelia. There is nothing to forgive. Now please take me home now!"

"Sharon I told you one time that I was taking you home to our house."

"Derrick quit playing, now take me home!"

"You know I never lied to you about having my house renovated. My Mom moved up here to Charlotte around eight years ago with my step dad. I decided last year I would renovate my house."

"So your parents moved up here and gave you the house?"

"Hell no! The house was always mine. My dad brought the house for me. The deed had my name on it when I was five years old. My Mom was executor over it until I turned twenty one. Now it is solely in my name."

"Derrick do you think it is fair to me that you are making me go somewhere I don't want to go?"

"Once you get down there and get used to it then you will love it."

"Derrick I can't just leave my family, and my job and not tell anyone where I am. They will be worried! My Mom will freakout!"

"She will be alright!"

"No… she won't. What would your Mom think if you just disappeared?"

"I don't know, my Mom always seems to know where I am at even if I don't want her to."

"Derrick we are almost at the South Carolina line, you need to get off 77 to 485 to take me home. What do you think will happen when they find my car still downtown in the parking garage? They will assume that I have been kidnapped or something and they will look for me."

"How can I kidnap my own wife? We eloped, and moved to my house in Sumter."

"I know you are not talking about Sumter South Carolina! Derrick how does that sound nobody will believe that. I just up and married a man I have not been seeing for months. I just left my job and family, gave no notice. I would rather die than marry you."

"Be careful what you ask for! Would you rather your niece and nephew die than to marry me?"

"Derrick you wouldn't dare!"

"Yes I would and I would do Brian's little brat too. They would all suddenly have an accident."

"You are crazy! You leave them out of this!"

"I will leave them out of this as long as you do what you are supposed to do."

"Why do you want to marry someone that doesn't love you?

"God showed me that we are supposed to be together. You will love me eventually."

"How can I love someone that kidnapped me, threatened my family, and trying to force me to marry him?"

"You will trust me."

"It's kind of hard to trust someone like you, besides I am in love with Brian, and that is who I want to marry."

"Well you'll get over it."

"You are crazy!"

"Hi Mom, where are the kids? I'm ready to go. This was a tough night, and I am glad I am off this weekend. Mom! Mom! Mom!"

"I'm sorry Wanda I didn't hear you, but the kids are in the den."

"Mom what's wrong?"

"Sharon called a few hours ago asking if I was at the hospital because Terell was
in a school bus accident."

"What would make her think that?"

"I don't know, and when I tried to ask her the phone went dead."

"Did you try calling her back?"

"Yes it went straight to voicemail."

"Did you try her job maybe she was getting in the elevator or something?"

"Yes we called her job, and they said she was not there. I have been calling her phone for the past two hours and it has been going to voicemail."

"Have you called the house?"

"Yes, and your father is on his way over there."

"Have you called Brian to see if she is with him, or if he has heard from her?"

"Yes, he said that he talked to her earlier, and they were supposed to go out tonight, and he hasn't heard from her. He came by and dropped off Felicia, and he is on his way downtown to see if she has her car."

"Have you called the police?"

"Yes, but they said she has not been gone long enough to be considered missing."

"Do you want me to take the kids home?"

"No, do you mind if they stay here a little while. I don't want to sit in the house by myself."

"Okay, I am going to pick up a couple of things for the kids. I also want to check to see if Sharon called and left a message."

"Please call me and let me know if you find out anything."

"Okay I will and Mom are you going to be alright? I can stay here if you like."

"No sweetheart I will be alright. Please go home to check to see if Sharon called, and pick up the things the kids will need."

"Okay, I'll call you in a little bit."

(Knock, knock)

"Come in!"

"Hey Shelia, what's going on?"

"You know what's going on! Your sister couldn't stand to see me with Derrick! She just had to have 'em."

"Shelia what are you talking about? Right now we don't even know where Sharon is. Sharon is missing and I don't have time for any of your drama!"

"Yea whatever, like you don't know, they are getting married."

"Shelia what the hell are you talking about? Sharon is not interested in Derrick. Sharon is in love with Brian. Who told you that, and what happened to your neck? OMG! Shelia what is wrong?"

"Nothing, just hope your sister gets everything she deserves!"

"Shelia, who told you that they were getting married?"

"I can't say anything. I have already said to much as it is."

"Look girl my sister maybe missing and like I said I don't have time for the drama. Now who told you that Sharon and Derrick were getting married?"

"Derrick told me. He says that he and Sharon have worked things out, and they will get married. When I threaten to confront Sharon he choked me. He told me he would kill me if I said anything to anybody."

"Shelia I am so sorry. Did you call the police?"

"No! He said he would kill me, and the way he looked at me when he said it I really believe him. Wanda I am not calling the police. It was not my fault I should have never threaten him."

"Shelia if you would have called the police, then they would have been looking for him, and he probably wouldn't have my sister!"

"How do you know he has her? How do you know that she didn't go willingly with him? How do you know that she wasn't still in love with him? How do you know that she just didn't go out of town?"

"OMG! I can't believe that you are sitting here defending this man. Sharon was never in love with Derrick. She let him go! You should be thanking God that Derrick left you. He could have killed you. Now if he did that to you what do you think he will do to my sister!"

"You don't even know if Derrick has her. Sweet little Sharon could be out getting her freak on."

"Or Derrick could have her. Shelia you don't know what he is capable of. You are right he might not have her, but we have to cover all basis. I will get things to take over to Mom's house and I will stay over there until we hear from Sharon so I will talk to you later."

"I came over here because I needed to talk to you and you're blowing me off. Everything is not about your sister!"

"You're right Shelia everything is not about my sister, but it is right now. The world doesn't revolve around you either. Now any other time I would sit and listen to your problems and issues, but now is not a good time."
"Whatever Wanda, I am outta here!"

I don't know what is wrong with her. I tell her that my sister maybe missing, and all she can think about is Derrick. I need to find me a different class of people to hang out with. Unwillingly is the only way Derrick could get Sharon to go with him. I don't see him making a scene in public. Maybe she went out after work with coworkers. I think that I am jumping to conclusion, but why would Derrick tell Shelia he and Sharon got back together and would be married? I just got this feeling he has my sister.

"Derrick I'm hungry. Can we stop and get something to eat?"
"I have plenty of food at the house and we will be there in about 30 minutes. I am sure you can wait."
"Why is it taking so long to get there? Sumter is only an hour and a half away!"

"I took the long way. I wanted to make sure that it was dark when we got here."

"Derrick, do you really expect for me to stay at your house with you?

"You mean our house and yes I do."

"My family will be wondering where I am."

"I got that covered. You will call them when you get to the house."

"What am I supposed to tell them?"

"Exactly what I tell you to."

"And what is that?"

"You will know when I want you to know."

"Mom."

"Yes dear."

"I just spoke to Shelia and she says Derrick told her that he and Sharon has got back together and are getting married. Did you know anything about this?"

"No, far as I know Brian is the only person that she is seeing. I don't believe that Sharon would not start back seeing Derrick."

"Me either, I know how she feels about Brian, and she would not just decide to go back with Derrick. Have you heard from Brian?"

"Yes, he went by the bank and her car is still in the parking garage."

"So what do we do now?"

"I don't know. Your father will be home in a minute. Maybe that's him calling now hold on. Hello."

"Mom."

"Sharon! Where are you?"

"I am out of town."

"Out of town where? Why didn't you tell someone you were going out of town?"

"I am sorry about that Mom, but that's why I am calling. I realized that I forgot to tell you and that's why I am calling. Tell Wanda I won't be getting the kids this weekend like I promised."

"Okay, but when will you be back?"

"I'll be back sometime next week."

"What about Brian? Are you going to call him?"

"Yes I will call him later on this weekend."

"What is this I hear about you and Derrick getting back together, and are getting married?"

"Mom I got to go tell Dad we will have dinner when I get back and I am sorry to cancel on him."

"Okay baby. You gave us a scare. Have you spoken to Derrick?"

"Mom I got to go. Me and a few friends are at a seafood restaurant getting ready to place our order, going to get me a lobster dinner with crab legs and shrimp. I am hungry I will call you later, bye."

"Sharon! Sharon! Sharon!"

"Wanda."

"Mom what's wrong?"

"That was Sharon hold on your father just came home."

"What did she say? Where is she?"

"I don't know. She just said that she forgot to tell us she was going out of town, says that she will be back sometime next week."

"I don't understand. Did she even tell you who she was with? What did she say when you asked her if she had spoken to Derrick?"

"Nothing, she just kept changing the subject when I asked her about Derrick."

"She told me to tell her father that she is sorry that she had to cancel dinner plans and that she will make it up to him when she gets back."

"Laura I didn't have any plans to have dinner with Sharon."

"Well honey that is what she said. She also told me to tell Wanda she is sorry that she can't get the kids this weekend."

"Okay this is weird because I have not talked to Sharon about getting the kids this weekend."

"Not as weird as what she said before she got off the phone."

"What did she say Mom?"

"That she was at the restaurant with some friends and that she was going to order her a lobster dinner with some crab legs and shrimps because she is hungry."

"Mom, Sharon is allergic to seafood!"

"I know! That's why I said it was weird."

"Laura I think our baby is in trouble and she was trying to tell us something."

"Mom, Dad do either of you know where Derrick lives?"

"No!"

"Let me make a call."

"Hello."

"Hey, Shelia do you know where Derrick lives?"

"No, he always stays at my house why?"

"Okay thanks."

"Wanda what's going on?"

"I'll tell you later I got to go."

"Laura, honey I am going to the church. Maybe they have some information about his address in the church records."

Chapter 13

"Derrick where are you?"

"I am out and about why?"

"I haven't heard from you all day. You didn't come home last night. Just wondering if everything is alright?"

"Everything is fine. Soon everything will be perfect."

"Derrick what's going on? Where are you?"

"I'll talk to you later bye."

"Hello."

"Hey Laura how are you?"

"I'm fine Edna, but I can't talk right now! We kind of have a family emergency."

"What's going on?"

"Sharon is missing and we don't know where she is."

"How long has she been gone?"

"She's been missing since yesterday afternoon."

"Have you heard from her?"

"Yes sort of. She called to say that she was out of town, but she wouldn't say where."

"Well she is not missing then, you have heard from her."

"But she didn't sound right and she didn't make any sense. We tried to ask her about Derrick, but she wouldn't say anything about him and she kept changing the subject."

"What does Derrick have to do with it? Why you asking her about him?"

"Because Derrick told somebody that he and Sharon had gotten back together and are going to get married."

"How do you know that's not true? She might have seen the error of her ways and realized that Derrick is the better man for her."

"Well she would not do that without speaking to Brad or me first."

"Well maybe she doesn't tell you everything. Yall need to quit thinking that Sharon is so perfect."

"We don't think she's perfect. We know our children make mistakes just like everyone else, and they make their own decisions. I know she would not get back with Derrick and just not say anything to anybody especially Brian. We did not teach our children to be inconsiderate of other people feelings."

"Well she doesn't seem to be to considerate about your feelings right now."

"Okay Edna it's time we get off the phone I will talk to you later."

Let me call Derrick to see if he has Sharon. He would not do anything that crazy. If he has I don't know how I can help him with this one.

"Derrick is Sharon with you?"

"Why would you ask me that?"

"Derrick just answer the question, is Sharon with you?"

"Why are you asking me if Sharon with me?"

"Because they seem to think that she is missing and that you got her! If she is with you is she there on her own free will?"

"What kind of question is that? What is it that you are trying to say?"

"Just answer the damn question!"

"Hello Derrick, Derrick!" I know that boy didn't just hang up on me!

(Knock, knock)

"Come in."

"Good evening Pastor may I talk to you for a minute?"

"Sure Deacon Hemphill. Do you need me to ask Elder Clarke to leave?"

"No he can stay maybe he has some insight on my problem."

"Okay deacon you got my attention, what's going on?"

"Well we believe that our daughter Sharon is in some kind of trouble. She left work the other day and we just heard from her this afternoon, and she kept saying things that didn't make any sense, and we believe she was trying to tell us something."

"Things like what deacon?"

"First she said she was sorry for cancelling our dinner plans. We did not have any dinner plans. Then she said that she was going out to eat at a seafood restaurant, and she is allergic to seafood."

"How do you know that she was not going to order something else?"

"Because she made it a point Elder to tell us that she would be ordering crab legs and shrimps."

"Calm down deacon has Sharon ever went off like this before?"

"No Sharon has kind of a ritual when she leaves to go out of town. She forwards her calls to our house. She usually lets her sister use her car so she can come by her house to pick the mail and just to check on things. Sharon would never just leave her car in a parking garage at her job."

"I think someone tricked her into going with them."

"Why would you say that?"

"Because Sharon called upset Friday afternoon saying that her nephew had been in a school bus accident and she was on the way to the hospital. She called Laura to inquire about it, and Laura told her the kids were there and then her phone went dead."

"That does sound kind of suspicious. Did you call the police?"

"Yes, they said because we have heard from her she is technically not missing. We think she is with Brother Derrick."

"Are you trying to say that Derrick has kidnapped your daughter?"

"No, we think that he might have tricked her to leave with him."

"That's the same thing. How do you know she is not out of town with friends? You are so ready to accuse one of your brothers and you know that is not right deacon."

"Okay let's calm down. Elder Clarke let me speak to Deacon Hamilton alone."

"But Pastor I cannot stand by and let him drag Brother Derrick's name through the mud. What if this gets out, people will talk. You cannot allow someone's reputation be ruin over speculation."

"I understand Elder, and you know I would not allow that to happen. I need to speak to the deacon as a worried and concerned father. I know you can understand that he is just worried about his baby girl."

"Yes sir I guess so."

Let me call Edna to check this story out. I will see if she heard from Brother Derrick. I hope he has nothing to do with this. No man would take a woman against their will at least no men I know. If he did I don't know what the boy is thinking about.

"Hey Edna where is Derrick?"

"I don't know why?"

"Have you heard from him lately?"

"No, what's going on James?"

"Do you know anything about him supposedly taking Sharon, or they are supposed to be together?"

"Yeah, and I have already straighten Laura out about that. How did you hear about it?"

"Brad is in the Pastor's office talking to him about it. He is trying to get a location of where Derrick lives, so he can check to see if Sharon is there."

"What does Derrick know about his real father?"

"I told him that his father died in the military. I had to tell so many lies fooling around with you. You should have owned up to it a long time ago. If your wife couldn't accept it then maybe she was not the person you should have married."

"Like I said what's done is done now. You know what that situation was like. Her father was the Pastor of the church we were attending and I was already engaged at the time."

"Yeah but that didn't stop you from sleeping around!"

"You know that I didn't sleep around. I just wasn't ready to be a father."

"Ready or not you still should have stood up to your responsibility."

"Again what's done is done."

"That nonchalant attitude is why we are in this mess. The sins of the father baby!"

"Just give me Derrick's number maybe I can talk to him."

"And say what?"

"No, I think it is a little too late for that. I will just talk to him."

"Derrick how long do you plan to keep me here?"

"Sharon please don't bother me with trivial things. I am trying to plan our wedding tomorrow."

"Derrick I am not going to marry you!"

"We will see, hold on while I answer the phone."

"Hello."

"Hello Derrick this is Elder Clark. Can I talk to you for a moment?"

"Hold on a minute. Sharon I will take this call because I am curious of what this joker has to say. Now I have to cover your mouth just in case you try to make any noise."

"Whatever Derrick."

"Hello Elder Clark how may I help you?"

"I just want to know if we can get together and talk."

"About what?"

"Just wanted to talk to you about the ministries that you are interested in. I also wanted to know if you would mind if I mentored you."

"I appreciate that, but I am out of town right now. I will call you when I get back."

"Oh okay. Are you out of town alone, or are you with someone?"

"What does that have to do with anything? Why don't you just say what it is you really want to know?"

"I was just asking, you know as men of God and holding a position in the church we have to be careful of what kind of situations that we put ourselves in."

"You are one to talk, because you don't have any room to talk to me about that!"

"What is that supposed to mean? Now it's time for you to say what you really want to say."

"Nothing I got to go. I have things I need to tend to."

"Okay, well we will talk when you get back. I really got things I need to talk to you about."

"Yea too little too late, but okay."

"I guess you are not going to tell me what you mean by that comment either."

"Mr. Clark we will talk when or if I come back."

Lord Derrick has Sharon with him. The question is, is she there willingly. I bet Edna knows more than she is telling. She was always protecting that boy. I pray that Sharon is safe and that no harm hurt or danger would come to her.

Chapter 14

"Brad how did it go?"

"The church was of no help with the address because they really didn't know if it was ethical to give me information on Brother Derrick."

"Brad this is our child!"

"Honey I know, but you have to see it from the church's point of view. The church don't want to be put in the middle. I have talked to Brian and he is on his way over."

"What are you going to do?

"Look Laura I just want you to trust me, and just let me handle this. I will need you to support me."

"Of course Brad I will support you, but please tell me what you are going to do."

"Brian is going to sit down and tell the children, while Wanda and I go to the parking deck to pick up Sharon's car."

"Brad I don't think we should tell the children, I don't want to scare them, or upset them."

"Laura sweetheart you don't think the children don't already know that something is going on. They haven't heard from or seen their aunt Sharon all weekend. Trust me honey they know something is going on."

"We are going to have the children work on the computer while we are gone to pick up the car. Brian will have them see if they can find any information on Derrick on the internet."

"Brad do you think there will be information on him?"

"I don't know honey, but we have to try something."

"Okay if you feel like the children are old enough to hear this I will support you."

"Hey grandma."

"Hello Felicia, how are you sweetheart?"

"Fine, where is Paw Paw?"

"He went out for a minute. He will be right back. Tawanda and Terell are in the den if you want to join them."

"Okay."

"Brain would you like something to eat or drink?"

"No thank you Mrs. Laura."

"Brian you don't have to be so formal. You see your daughter has adjusted and dropped the formalities."

"Yes, she has taken to your family."

"Yes, she has. So when are you going to take to the family?"

"I have taken to you all. Love you like you were my own family."

"Brian we are your family. The next time I should hear you call me Mom."

"Yes ma'am."

"So are you going to tell the children when Brad gets here?"

"No actually I am going to tell them now. He wanted me to start before he gets here."

"Okay do you want me to go in there with you?"

"Yes, please."

"Children I need to talk to you about something very important. It is about your aunt Sharon."

I looked down at wide eyes and knew this would not be easy. Children are sensitive and very aware of their surroundings and the atmosphere. They can always tell when something is wrong. I thought it would be better for us to tell them than to have them guess and seeing us upset. Tawanda was the first to speak.

"Uncle Brian what is wrong with Aunt Sharon?"

"Well it seems that we don't know where she is."

"Well why don't you call her cell phone?"

"We tried that Terell and she is not answering."

"Dad do you think Sharon will be okay?"

"Yes. Sharon is a smart girl, and she knows that we are doing everything that we can on our end. She is probably thinking of some things that she can do also."

"So yes I do think she will be okay."

"Daddy, have you called Amanda?"

"Yes they are coming over. Your mother has been cooking all day. Wanda she has enough food there to feed the US Army."

"Yeah I know Mom cooks when she is nervous."

"Thank God she is not nervous all the time, because we would be as big as the house."

"Dad how are we going to find Sharon?"

"Baby I have been praying about it, and God is going to show us a way."

"Well I wish He would hurry up."

"Girl you can't rush God. Everything is in His timing.

"Sharon I have planned a very special night for us."

"What is so special about tonight?"

"We are celebrating our pre wedding night."

"Derrick please just let me go. I will call home and ask someone to come and get me. Matter of fact you can just drop me off at the train or bus station."

"Now why would I do that I told you before that we were going to be married. God has shown me that you were going to be my wife."

"God has not shown me that you are going to be my husband."

"That's because you are not open enough for God to reveal it to you."

"Derrick we can't even get along. You have kidnapped me. Do you think God is a part of that?"

"God knows I did what I had to do to carry out His will for me and you."

"There is no sense in talking to you anymore. You only hear what you want to hear."

(Knock, knock)

"So I see that you are expecting company. What do you think that I am supposed to do while you entertain company? I am not going to just stay up here and be quiet. I want out of this room, and I want to go home!"

"I don't know who that could be. No one knows that we are here. I am going to cover you're month again, but I will be right back."

"Who is it?"

"Elder Clark."

"What the hell are you doing here?"

"I took a guess that you would be here. We need to talk."

"Well I'm here what do you want?"

"Aren't you going to invite me in?"

"No. I know, and you know how you knew where I would be. You should, considering you paid for this house."

"So you know that I am your father?"

"Of course I know. I have known for years."

"Can I come inside so we can talk about this?"

"No, you can't. I am busy right now."

"Do you have company?"

"So what if I do? But since you asked no I don't have company."

"Then what was that noise then?"

"None of your business. You may have paid for the house, but it is still in my name."

"Listen Derrick I know that I should have been more of a father to you, but what is done is done. I can't go back and change the past. What is that noise? Sounds like someone is knocking something over upstairs!"

"It's nothing now leave, before I call the police. I don't want you anywhere near me or my property again."

"But I am only trying to help you."

"What is it that you think that I need help with? Don't you think you are a little late to play daddy.

"Maybe so but it doesn't change the fact that I am still your father, and I am trying to help you. I don't want you to do something stupid that could ruin your life."

"Something stupid! Like having a baby and denying he exist? Do you mean stupid like killing a woman's spirit that was in love with you by breaking her heart and marrying someone else that kind of stupid?"

"Listen Derrick, when I was seeing your mother I never made any promises to her."

"Yeah, but you knew she was in love with you!"

"Derrick please listen to me. Don't do this! Please allow me to take Sharon back with me. If you continue with this I won't be able to bail you out on this one."

"When did you bail me out of anything?"

"I know you haven't forgotten the mess with your first wife. If it hadn't been for me you would have been locked up. I had to call in a lot of favors in order to get those charges dropped. You didn't think that your problems magically disappeared."

"Nigga get the hell out of my house! I don't need your trifling ass. You are supposed to be a deacon, but you kept a secret child hidden so it wouldn't tarnish your image. Get the hell out of my house NOW!

This did not turned out how I hoped that it would. I knew I heard something or someone in the house. I will have to call Deacon Hemphill and have him come down here. If Sharon is not there it will at least give him a peace of mind to know that Derrick doesn't have her.

"Hello."

"Deacon Hemphill, this is Elder Clark. I need for you to come down to Sumter, SC."

"How can I help you Elder? I am busy trying to find my daughter."

"I think I know where she is."

"How can you possibly know where she is?"

"Deacon you are going to have to just trust me."

"Okay Elder. Where is she?"

"Down here in South Carolina. How long will it take you to get here?

"Brian and I will be there in about an hour."

"I don't think it will be a good idea to bring Brian."

"Why not?"

"Cause if Derrick has her, it would not be a good if he sees Brian."

"What do you mean if Derrick has her? I thought you already knew where my daughter is."

"Deacon you think Derrick had something to do with Sharon's disappearance?"

"Yes I do."

"Okay I know where Derrick is and I have talked to him. If you believe that Derrick has her then you will come down here."

"Okay I will come, but Brian is still coming with me."

"Alright I will meet you at the gas station near his house. Let me give you the address."

"Honey we are on our way out. We will be back in a little while"

"Brad where are you going?"

"We have a lead on where Derrick is and we are going to follow up on it."

"Brian you ready?"

"Yes sir, I am."

"Brad you can't just leave without telling me what is going on."

"Laura I will tell you on the way down there."

"On the way down where?"

"South Carolina."

"What!"

"Look Laura I will call you in a minute."

"Okay, but I am looking for your call and if I don't get it in a few minutes than I am going to call you!"

"Okay, baby I will talk to you in a minute."

Brian and I jumped in the car to head down 77 south. I was trying to keep my nerves calm, but it was hard. All I could think about is what he could do to her or already done.

"Mr. Hemphill did you tell Mrs. Laura everything that you know?"

"No not really just enough to satisfy her curiosity."

"Do you want to tell me anything? I mean I am going down here with you, and I don't know what kind of situation that I am walking into."

"You're right Brian, but I wish I had more information for you. I guess I should have asked Elder Clark how he knew where Derrick was, but my main concerned is Sharon right now."

"I understand. I didn't know that Elder Clark was helping you look for her."

"That makes two of us. I don't know how he knew where to look, when I couldn't find out anything from the church."

"Well I guess you can ask him. We will be there in the next 20 minutes."

"Yeah I know, but Brian the real reason I asked you here. Something just don't feel right about the whole situation."

"Yeah I know I was thinking the same thing. I have this feeling that just won't go away."

"Yeah, me too."

Lord help me to understand what is going on. I pray that we find my little girl safe with no harm, hurt, or danger to her. Please send the Holy Spirit down to comfort her, and let her know that we miss her and are praying for her. I ask this in Jesus name. Amen.

Lord please forgive me for all that I have done. I thank you for your mercy and your grace that endureth forever. Lord please help Derrick to understand that I did this to help him. I really don't want him to think that I called Sharon's father to betray him. I am to blame for a lot of what is going on with him. I really want to make amends for everything that I have done to him. Father please forgive me for all the mistakes I have made.

"Sharon I have a surprise for you."
"Derrick where have you been? You left me up in this room for hours, and I am hungry."
"I went out to get us something to eat. I went to get your favorite food."
"What?"
"I wanted to surprise you with a seafood feast tonight, so I went to Red Lobster to get us a feast to celebrate our pre-wedding night.
"Derrick I can't eat seafood. I am allergic to it."
"That's not what you said on the phone to your parents."
"I know, but trust me I have a bad reactions to seafood."
"Well this is all I brought so I guess you need to decide how hungry you really are."

"If you want to starve then you do that. I am getting ready to set up in here and the food will be here if you would like it. We are getting ready to sit down and discuss our future. Now I will be back."

This man is trying to kill me. I can't eat this food. I am allergic and I will have a bad reaction. I am hungry, but I am not that hungry. I see rolls so I will just eat those.

That looks like Deacon Hemphill pulling up now. I hope he don't ask too many questions because right now is not the time for an interrogation.

"Hey Elder Clark."

"Hey Deacon. Glad you came."

"Elder tell me what is going on."

"Well I talked to Derrick and he says that he did not take Sharon."

"I take it you don't believe him?"

"No. I kept hearing something in the house. It sounded like something being knocked over."

"He says it was a cat, but Derrick is allergic to cats."

"Excuse me Elder Clark I know that we don't know each other well, but how do you know that Derrick is allergic to cats."

"Well Brian that is something that I just know."

"Elder you know a lot more than you are telling me. I don't have time for games. My little girl is missing, so whatever game you are playing with Derrick I don't have time for it."

"Deacon, Derrick is my son."

"What?"

"That's right Derrick is my son. I have not been in his life, but I know everything about him."

"I didn't know that you and Clara had children."

"We don't. I got Derrick's Mom pregnant before I married Clara."

"I didn't know at the time that Clara couldn't bear any children so I never told her about Derrick and never acknowledged him."

"So this is how you know where he is."

"Yes, I brought this house for him when he was younger. He was not supposed to know that I brought it. The house was in his name since he was a young boy. He was raised by his aunt, and she never let me forget it."

"Okay where is he?"

"He is just five minutes away."

"Okay, let's go."

"Wait a minute Deacon. Please listen to the rest of my story before we go. I feel like a big burden is being lifted by telling someone. I don't want your pity, or anger. I just need for you to listen, so you can understand what Derrick is going through."

"Listen James and yes I am calling you by your name because I don't consider you an Elder. I don't care what Derrick is going through! He is the least of my concerns. My only concern is for my daughter!"

"Look you need to know his state of mind. He thinks he loves Sharon, so I don't think she is in real danger right now."

"Okay Elder. I will only listen if you make it quick so we can get my daughter."

"Well you have to understand I was seeing my wife at the same time that I was seeing Derrick's Mom. I knew that Clara was the one I would marry because I had already asked her when I met Derrick's Mom. Clara's father was the Pastor of the church I was attending. He was my mentor and his opinion of me mattered a lot. I liked Derrick's Mom a lot, but we both knew that we were out to have a good time, or at least I thought we were."

"James you were seeing two women at a time?"

"Yes, but I wasn't an Elder then."

"And that makes it alright because you weren't an Elder?"

"No that's not what I am saying. I was young and that is not an excuse either."

"Look just finish the story."

"Well Derrick's Mom got pregnant, and I was very upset. I was getting married and she tells me she is pregnant. I tried to talk her into terminating her pregnancy, but she would not hear of it. Derrick was born and I sent money to her for him. Derrick's Mom didn't want money, she wanted to be with me. She committed suicide. Now Derrick was around five when that happened, and he went to stay with his aunt. She tortured me for years. I brought him a house and had it put in his name. That is how I knew where to find him."

"Okay what happened to the aunt, and is that why he moved up to Charlotte?"

"I don't know. I was shocked when he showed up. That is when Edna approached me to nominate him for a Deacon position."

"What does Sister Edna have to do with this?"

"She is his aunt."

"What?"

"She never said a word about Derrick being her nephew."

"Well he called her Mom for so many years that she didn't know that he knew about his real Mom, or about me. Derrick has had a lot of problems over the years. He has been in a mental hospital, due to some issues he was dealing with."

"Don't you mean issues that he is still dealing with? How come you or Edna never mentioned you were related to Derrick? Now he may have my daughter and neither one of us knows what he can do."

"He is still my son, and I know he would not do something like that. He would never hurt her. He loves her."

"No you don't know him. Have you ever spent time with him? You and Edna are the reason we are in this mess. Had you said something before, now my daughter would not be with a lunatic right now. Edna pushed them together."

"You can't blame Edna. She has dedicated her life to taking care of and protecting Derrick."

"Grown men don't need protecting. All I know is that if something happens to my daughter you and Edna will pay for it!"

"Come on Mr. Hemphill let's just find Sharon. Elder Clark where does Derrick live?"

"I will show you. I am not letting you go over there without me."

"Well let's go!"

Chapter 15

"Derrick you know you can't keep me here forever. Just let me go. How do you expect for us to have a marriage with me locked up in a room?"

"I will unlock the door once we are married."

"How do you know that I will stay?"

"Well if you don't I have a way that will ensure that we will be together forever."

"What way is that?"

"Let's just say until death do us part will be taken literally."

"What are you trying to say?"

"You know what I am trying to say. If we can't be together in marriage, then we will be together in death."

"Derrick please don't do this. I know you don't want to die. I know I don't want to die. Please, please Derrick let me go!"

"The only way I will let you go is in death."

"Derrick why are you doing this?"

"Because I love you and we are destined to be together."

"You call this love? This is not the way you show someone you love them."

"It may not be the way that you show them, but it is my way to show you. Did you know that my Mom committed suicide over love? The only mistake she made is that she should have taken him with her."

"That's not a good thing to say. I am sorry about your Mom, but that doesn't mean you have to have the same fate. Derrick think about what you are doing. This can ruin your life."

"Not if I am not alive to worry about it. Now do you plan to eat with me or are you going to make me eat alone?"

Lord please help me. I praying for you to give me the strength to get through this situation. Lord give me the words to make Derrick understand what he is doing is wrong. Help me reach him, and make him realize there is a better way. Lord I don't want to marry him, and I don't want to die. Lord please help me.

"Why are you crying?"

"I don't want to be here. I want to go home to my family."

"I am your family now, so come on eat something."

Lord he doesn't seem to understand that I am allergic to seafood. I will eat because I am hungry. If anyone will decide how I leave this earth it may as well be me. Well here I go.

"Sharon what's wrong? Why are you swelling up?"

"Told you I was allergic to seafood."

"Why did you eat it?"

"Damn now someone is at the door. What the hell is going on? This is not the way it is supposed to happen."

"Who is it?"

"It's Clark!"

"What do you want I told you that we have nothing to say to each other?"

"Derrick please open the door!"

"What!"

"Derrick where is my daughter?"

"Mr. Hemphill, what are you doing here?"

"Looking for my daughter!"

"What makes you think that she is here?"

"Where else would she be? You have been after her for months. Now she has found someone else to be with and you don't like it."

"Okay and that means what? I brought her up here against her will, to do what?"

"I don't know what is going on in your sick head."

"I am not leaving until I am satisfied that she is not here."

"I will just call the police and we will see what they have to say."

"Go ahead call the police, because I would like to see what they have to say also."

"What is that noise? It is coming from upstairs. Sharon baby is that you? Daddy is coming!"

"Wait you can't just bust into my house!"

"Oh my God! Clark call 911 she is having an allergic reaction. Brian we have to get her to a hospital."

"You are not going anywhere. I will not let him take Sharon from me again. You have poisoned her mind against me and now she doesn't want to have anything to do with me."

"Derrick what are you doing! Put that gun down! What are you doing with a gun?"

"Dear old dad, how do you suppose that Mr. Hemphill knew where I was? You called him didn't you?"

"Derrick I only did that for your own good!"

"Did you tell him that I was you illegitimate son?"

"If you are asking if I told them that you are my son, yes I did!"

"You finally acknowledge that I am your son. Well it is too little too late."

"Derrick it is never too late. No one is leaving this house. Sharon and I will be married and you can just stay for the wedding or you can leave."

"Derrick I will not stand by and let you marry the woman that I love. I came here to get her, and I will leave with her."

"Brian I have no problem shooting you, because I never liked you anyway."

"Well the feeling is mutual."

"Brian please you are not making the situation any better."

"Doesn't matter Elder Clark. I am leaving with Sharon. If we don't get her to a hospital she will die."

"I hear the ambulance coming."

"Clark I hope you called the police when you call the ambulance?"

"No I just called the ambulance."

"What? Why didn't you call the police?"

"Brad he is my son!"

"Now we can handle this without getting the police involved."

"No we can't! Derrick is coming out of here in handcuffs."

"For what Brad? You don't know if he kidnapped her or not. She cannot speak for herself right now."

"Hold on! I don't need you speaking for me. You have not been my father all my life, and I don't need you speaking for me right now!"

"Derrick don't do anything crazy, please!"

"Crazy, crazy! You want to know what is crazy. When my Mom killed herself she should have taken you with her!"

"What are you saying?"

"When my mother killed herself, she should have also killed you, but I can easily rectify that!"

I stood there holding my breath not knowing what Derrick was going to do next. I can't believe that this situation has gotten so much out of hand. God please come down and …

"Derrick Nooooo!"

(Bang!)

Thank you all who have supported "When Church Is Over" your love and support was greatly appreciated. I have included inserts from "When Church Is Over 2" hope that enjoy.

When Church Is Over 2

Chapter 1

I had closed my eyes for a brief moment. I just knew that Derrick had shot me. If this is my fate I will accept it. I have repented for my sins and tried my best to make amends with Derrick as well as with my heavenly father.

Right now I was feeling no pain. Maybe my body went into shock and that the reason I don't feel anything.

I opened my eyes and I saw Derrick on the floor. I saw blood spilling over the carpet. I looked to check myself and realized I haven't been shot. I bent down to pray that God would spare my son. I felt myself being pushed out of the way. I look up and notice there were fireman and EMTs everywhere. I looked for Deacon Hemphill and he was nowhere to be found. I got up as they were putting Derrick and Brian on stretchers. Still had no idea who got shot I was thankful it wasn't me and I was also thankful it wasn't my son.

As I was walking down the stairs my mind was moving a mile a minute. I knew that I didn't have but a short window to try and defuse the situation and help Derrick. I knew from working with the law for so many years that the hospitals by law have report all gunshot incidents.

I rushed out to my car to follow the EMTs to the nearest hospital. I quickly pulled out my cell phone to make a call. The phone on the other end just rang. I knew she would answer so I just let it ring.

"Hello."

It felt so good to hear my sweet wife's voice. "Hi Sweetheart."

"James where are you?"

"I'm in South Carolina. One of our members had to be rushed to the hospital."

"Are they okay?"

"I don't know, but I will keep you updated."

"Please do. What is their name so I can be praying for them?"

"Baby. I'm sorry but the signal down here is bad. I will call you back as soon as I can." I quickly hung up the phone. I didn't want to have to lie to my wife. This was not the time to come clean about Derrick being my son.

I picked up the phone again to dial another number that I was dreading to call. As the phone rung my stomach was in knots. I knew Edna was going to be upset and start fussing about how out of hand this situation has gotten.

"James! What took you so long to call me? What the hell is going and where is Derrick?"

"Derrick is on the way to the hospital."

"Why The Hell is Derrick on the way to the hospital James?" You know what, never mind. Where exactly are you? I am on my way!"

"Edna I working on the situation."

"Well I can't tell because you are doing a piss poor job at it. I am still coming. Where the hell are you?"

"Edna please don't come down here and make the situation worst."

"James tell me how can it get any worse?"

"Edna let me do what I need to do."

"Okay what is it that you are going to do?"

"First I need to know how bad the situation is."

"I only have a small window before the police get involved, if you come down here making a scene that will only make things worse for me."

"James let's get one thing clear. I don't give a damn about making things worse for you. What I will do is give you one hour. If I don't hear from you in that hour then I will be down there."

"Fine Edna. I will call you within the hour."

I hate talking to her on the phone. That woman works my nerves. I hope that she don't come running down here making things worse for me or Derrick. As I parked the car I noticed that there were a couple of police officers stationed at the emergency room entrance. It seems that they don't waste any time. I just pray that they are here for security purposes. Derrick hasn't even gotten in the hospital good so how did they know to call the police.

I still don't know how I am going to spin this situation to get Derrick off. I am going to have to speak with Deacon Hemphill. I know he is furious and getting him to understand sending Derrick to jail will not do the situation any good.

As I was walking down the hall of Tuomey Regional Medical Center I was preparing myself for the conversation I was going to have with Brad. I knew that it was not going to go well. I will admit I am over protective of Derrick because I believe that he got the short end of the stick partly due to me. I have been doing all I can to fix it, and if it is the last thing that I do I will fix it. I will prove to my son that I am here for him.

I ran into the hospital up to the front desk. "Ma'am can you tell me what room that Sharon Hemphill is in?" I knew I didn't have much time and I knew that I should have been trying to find out what happened to Derrick first, but I need to see what Brad or Sharon was planning to say or do.

"Sir are you family?"

"No ma'am I am her Elder at the church."

"She is not in a room yet. She is down the hall."

I looked down the hall to where the nurse was pointing. I saw Brad pace up and down the corridor outside of Sharon's room. She looked pretty bad when they took her away. I pray that she has a speedy recovery.

"Hi Brad. How is Sharon doing?"

"Better no thanks to you and that demon seed of yours. They are stabilizing her now. They are going to keep her for a few days to make sure everything is okay."

"Now I'm going to let you have that one since you are concerned about your child. I told you that he wouldn't hurt her."

"You don't have to let me have nothing. All this mess is mostly your fault. You are a poor excuse for a man, and even a worst excuse as an elder."

"Brad now you are taking this too far. I am not the one that you want to mess with. I told you that there was need to get the police involved."

"Oh really? So you big and bad now. But you weren't so big and bad back in the day when you were making babies."

"Brad you don't want to go to war with me because I promise you will not win."

"First of all you don't scare, me and secondly I am not scared of going to war over my children."

"Brad I came to talk to calmly. Now we can work this out without getting the police involve."

"Man have you lost your mind! Derrick is going to jail! I turned away from James because I couldn't stand to look at him. The only thing that scares me is going to jail for knocking the hell out of this man. I turned back around and he was still standing there, I looked at him thinking what the hell does he want, but I didn't say it.

"Brad listen to me. This is what we tell the police. We are going to tell them that this is all a misunderstanding. That Derrick and Sharon was heading out of town for the weekend and she took in some for they had shell fish in it. She had an allergic reaction to the dinner. We all came down to check on them and Derrick thought that we were intruders and pulled out a weapon to protect them."

"James I will not be telling the police nothing but the truth."

"Brad how do you know that is not the truth. Sharon is in no condition to give a statement. She is lucky that she arrived at the hospital when she did. She could have died. All we have to do is tell the police that she is no in a condition to give a statement and they will back off."

"James listen to what you are saying. You are trying to excuse Derrick's behavior. Do you really think that this is going to help him? This is what is wrong with Derrick now. You and Edna have not made him take responsibility for any of his action so now he thinks that there are no consequences for any of his actions. Now move out of my way so I can meet my wife at the entrance when she gets here and prepare to speak with the police."

"Brad I am trying to save Sharon the heartache to come. Let's say Derrick is arrested and it goes to trail which I know if won't, but lets say that it does. They are going to ask why she got in the car with Derrick in the first place. If things are over with them as she stated then why get in the car with him. Is it that she is seeking attention, or trying to convince her dad because she knows that he doesn't like her boyfriend? See Brad I can spin any story. Now when Sharon called her Mom why didn't see tell her she was in trouble. I know that you say that she gave off clues, but why didn't she just Mom Derrick has kidnapped me? Anything she says I can tear it down. Look Brad we don't have to get the law involved. Let's work this out without getting the police involved. I will have Derrick committed to a mental hospital."

"Oh yea, and how long would he stay? Who would determine when he was better? Naw man we are going to play this out in the court."

"Brad this is not what you want to do."

"Yes it is. I need to make sure he is locked up and not able to hurt anyone else's daughter."

"Brad I won't allow my son to go to jail."

"How can you stop it? You may have a little clout in Charlotte, but these people don't know you down here."

"Brad why do you think I brought a house down here. I didn't just pick Sumter out of the blue. This is my home town. This is my stomping grounds. I am well known. See the difference between me and you is I always do my homework on everybody I come into contact with. The bible tells us that we parish because of lack of knowledge. I always make sure that I have as much knowledge as possible." Brad just stood there with his mouth hanging open. I know that he was shocked with that revelation. "Look Brad whether we are in Charlotte or Sumter I am not an enemy you want to have so I need you to let me handle this."

"Man you can't just come up in my face and punk me. You don't scare me."

"I'm not trying to scare you. I am just asking you to fall back and let me handle this."

"Naw I don't think I can do that."

"Okay have it your way."

"Remember James you don't shake no branches on this tree. You don't want me as an enemy either."

"I know I don't shake any branches on you tree. See I don't like to shake branch I prefer to cut the tree down.

Like I said I am not an enemy that you want to have, but it is one that you are going to get."

"Bring it on James. I may not have the clout that you seem to think that you have, but I can be very resourceful. I may not make that kind of money that you make, but I am very resourceful with the money that I did make. So don't think you are dealing with some weak man because you're not. I will be able to go toe to toe with you. Now you need to ask yourself would you like for me to dig all your skeletons out of your closet."

"Brad you need to tread carefully. Doesn't matter what skeletons are in my closet. I will repent for those sins and will be forgiven by God as well as by men at the least the men that count."

I just turned and walked away from him. It is a shame that James think that all he has to do is repent. God may forgive him, but he is still going to have to suffer the all the things that he has done and there will be consequences. As I was walking down the hall to get away from James I turned back to see that two police officers were approaching him. I quickly turned around and approached the three of them. As I approached I notice that the police officers were leaving. "Wait where are they going?"

"I told them that Sharon was not up to talking right now. I didn't want them in her room until she is stabilized. I am getting ready to head to my son's room to see how he is doing. I will talk to you later."

I watched him walk off as if there is nothing wrong with this situation. He acts as if everything is going work itself out. I don't know who is more delusional him or Derrick. I walked off to the front entrance to wake for my wife. They did not want Sharon to have visitors yet until they had her comfortable in her room.

Made in the USA
Middletown, DE
04 September 2015